Sherlock Holmes and the Adventure of the Ghost Machine

by

David MacGregor

First edition published in 2021
© Copyright 2021
David MacGregor

The right of David MacGregor to be identified as the author of this work has been asserted by him in accordance with the Copyright, Designs and Patents Act 1998.

All rights reserved. No reproduction, copy or transmission of this publication may be made without express prior written permission. No paragraph of this publication may be reproduced, copied or transmitted except with express prior written permission or in accordance with the provisions of the Copyright Act 1956 (as amended). Any person who commits any unauthorised act in relation to this publication may be liable to criminal prosecution and civil claims for damage.

All characters appearing in this work are fictitious. Any resemblance to real persons, living or dead, is purely coincidental. The opinions expressed herein are those of the author and not of Orange Pip Books.

Paperback ISBN 978-1-78705-717-3
ePub ISBN 978-1-78705-718-0
PDF ISBN 978-1-78705-719-7

Published by Orange Pip Books
335 Princess Park Manor, Royal Drive,
London, N11 3GX
www.orangepipbooks.com

Cover design by Brian Belanger

For Kelsey

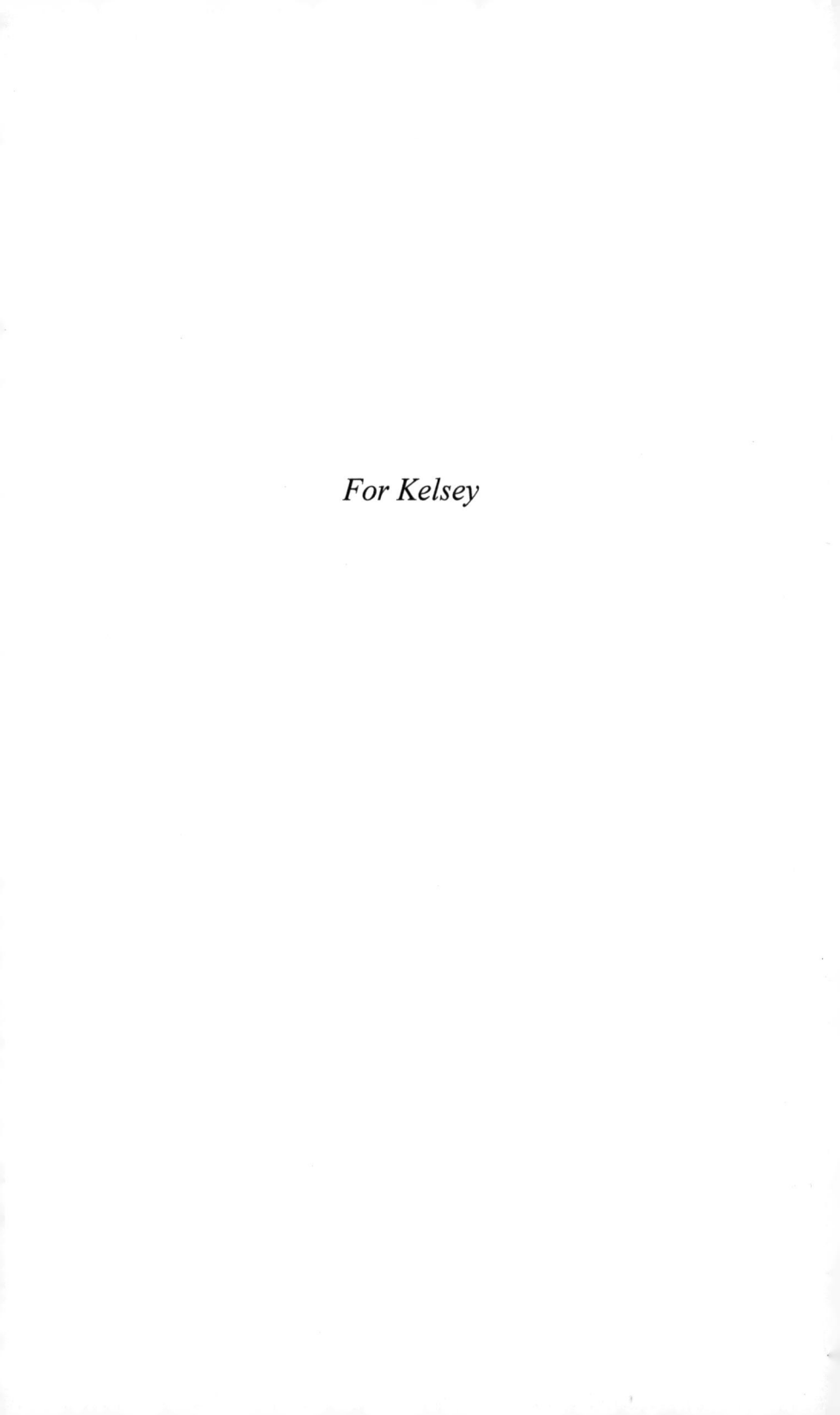

Acknowledgments

This story, along with its companion pieces, "Sherlock Holmes and the Adventure of the Elusive Ear" and "Sherlock Holmes and the Adventure of the Fallen Soufflé," began life as a play at The Purple Rose Theatre Company in Chelsea, Michigan. First and foremost, my eternal thanks goes to my friend and colleague Guy Sanville, who directed "Elusive Ear," and always pushes me to make the story better. My gratitude also goes toward the dozens of talented and highly skilled collaborators who made these plays successful. And of course, my thanks to actor, playwright, composer, and musician Jeff Daniels for founding The Purple Rose Theatre Company in 1991 and providing a home for innumerable artists.

Special thanks goes to Hope Shangle, who offered an attentive ear and thoughtful insights over coffee and pastries, then volunteered her considerable web wizard talents as needed. Thanks also to the Amateur Mendicant Society of Detroit and Holmesian guru Howard Ostrom, whose enthusiasm for this new version of Sherlock Holmes was deeply appreciated. My brother Iain MacGregor and good friend Peter Morris were kind enough to cast a careful eye over the text, and I am extremely grateful to Steve Emecz, Richard Ryan, and the team at MX Publishing for gracefully ushering these stories into a different medium and giving them an entirely new audience.

Finally, a deep and heartfelt bow to Sir Arthur Conan Doyle for creating, as Vincent Starrett poetically expressed it, "two men of note who never lived and so can never die."

Contents

Introduction	1
1. The Fallen Hero	5
2. The First Secret Invention	17
3. The Second Secret Invention	30
4. The Government Agent	44
5. The First Secret Revealed	57
6. The Second Secret Revealed	71
7. The Mysterious Mystery	84
8. A Most Peculiar Investigation	97
9. A Walking Tour of London	112
10. Preparations for a Séance	127
11. The Scientific Séance	142
12. The More Things Change…	155

Introduction

Despite being a medical doctor, I would never describe myself as a particularly scientific man. While I had dutifully slogged through my courses on biology and chemistry while at university, the scientific world had never excited my interest to any undue extent. As a physician, my focus was on helping my fellow man, whether in private practice or on the battlefield during my service in Afghanistan.

This usually involved setting broken bones, stitching up wounds, digging Jezail bullets out of my comrades, or prescribing medication for this or that ailment. However, it would never have occurred to me to invent a reagent to test for the presence of blood, as my friend Sherlock Holmes had done shortly after we met and as I related in "A Study in Scarlet." For whatever reason, I simply don't have that turn of mind.

However, with every passing day, it was now abundantly evident that the minds of many of my fellow citizens were most definitely devoted to experimentation and innovation. What had begun as a trickle of inventions in the middle of the nineteenth century had assumed the proportions of a veritable cataract, and one couldn't open a newspaper these days without reading about some astonishing new device or discovery.

Communication had become much easier thanks to the invention of the telegraph in 1837 and the telephone in 1876; transportation had been transformed, thanks to trains and then the invention of the automobile in 1889; and organization and tidiness had received its own godsend by way of the paperclip in 1899. Perhaps most astonishingly, only two years before the story I am about to relate took place, the Wright brothers had successfully flown the first aeroplane at Kitty Hawk, North

Carolina, and just last year Thomas Sullivan sent a shiver through every right-minded Englishman when he announced that he had invented the teabag.

Still, human nature being what it is, this outpouring of brilliance and enterprise did not mean that the consulting practice and talents of Sherlock Holmes had been consigned to oblivion. Far from it. Driven by ignorance, prejudice, and boundless greed, humanity simply developed different and more efficient ways to prey upon one another, all in the name of progress. Like the famous Dutch boy with his finger in the dike to prevent a deluge, Holmes held fast in his determination to uphold the values of truth and justice to the best of his ability, although it must be said in all candour that he seemed to have grown somewhat weary of this role as of late, taking more and more comfort in reading, obscure chemical experiments, and his relationship with Miss Irene Adler, the American opera singer, who initially came to our attention due to the fact that she was blackmailing the King of Bohemia (entirely due to his own monstrous behaviour, I might add).

For readers new to these posthumously published tales of Sherlock Holmes, I should explain that far from passing away after the conclusion of "A Scandal in Bohemia," Miss Adler had moved in with Holmes and I under the guise of being Mrs. Hudson, our housekeeper. Not to belabour the point any more than necessary, Holmes and Miss Adler had fallen madly in love with each other practically upon first sight, and although my nose was put a bit out of joint to find her belongings being unpacked in our rooms, I soon came to admire and respect her intelligence, discretion, and the manner in which she was able to keep Holmes grounded in ways that I never could. Faced with the necessity of explaining the constant presence of a woman on the premises, I simply presented her in the stories I wrote for "The Strand Magazine" as Mrs. Hudson, a neat little bit of invention which she didn't mind going along with.

Subsequently, Miss Adler had been of invaluable assistance in any number of cases, especially those that involved the brilliant and wicked daughter of the late Professor Moriarty—Marie Chartier—who had first come to our attention in "The Adventure of the Elusive Ear," when a bloodied and desperate Vincent Van Gogh had showed up on our doorstep. We had then matched wits with her again in "The Adventure of the Fallen Soufflé," a case that involved not only the scandal-ridden Prince of Wales, but also Auguste Escoffier, the most celebrated chef in the world.

I'm happy to say that Miss Adler's presence at 221B also had the edifying effect of expanding my musical horizons beyond the stylings of Gilbert and Sullivan to include the stirring marches of John Philip Sousa, as well as a number of catchy ditties from New York's Tin Pan Alley. I was especially fond of a new American composer, George M. Cohan, whose popular tune, "Give My Regards to Broadway," had caught my ear a week or two before the story you are about to read began.

As for this tale, I never for a moment considered writing it up for "The Strand Magazine." My Edwardian readers would have been shocked to the core at some of the revelations herein, and His Majesty's government would have insisted that a number of crucial sections be removed in the interest of national security. Still, as it does present several features of interest insofar as the career of Sherlock Holmes is concerned, upon completion I plan on consigning it to my battered despatch box at Cox and Company for the delectation of future generations, should it ever see the light of day at all. I sincerely hope it does, for I believe it shows my good friend Sherlock Holmes at both his best and his worst; in short, at his most human.

(Editor's Note: In the original Sherlock Holmes stories, astute historians noted occasional factual errors and timeline discrepancies, which were invariably put down to the unreliability of Dr. Watson. This tendency did not diminish as the good Doctor entered his later years, but it does not detract in any meaningful way from the pleasure to be had in this long-hidden tale from the annals of Sherlock Holmes.)

Chapter One
The Fallen Hero

London: November 29, 1905.

As it turned out, Bernard Darwin is a damned good egg. And yes, when I refer to Bernard Darwin, I am speaking of none other than the grandson of the great English naturalist, Charles Darwin himself. Things had been particularly slow at 221B of late, and so on the evening in question I took myself out to the Royal Society to listen to a lecture on Darwin by his quite accomplished son, Francis. Rather surprised and delighted to find myself seated next to Bernard, Francis' son, we got to talking and I quickly discovered that Bernard was an avid reader of my Sherlock Holmes stories. This alone marked him as a man of nice judgement and good taste, and while I would have been interested to learn more about his upbringing and experiences in such a remarkable family, I was too busy answering his quite perceptive and intelligent questions regarding "The Five Orange Pips" and "The Adventure of the Second Stain."

The lecture itself was, as you might expect, fascinating in the extreme, with Francis offering any number of insights and anecdotes related to Charles Darwin's life and work. Apparently, Charles had intended to become a doctor, just like his father, up until the day that he realised he couldn't stand the sight of blood. He also had an aversion to eating owls, a titbit of information that seemed to raise more questions than it answered. Following the lecture, as I collected my coat, I felt a tug on my elbow and turned to find Bernard at my side.

"What now, Watson, old fellow?" he asked. "Back to Baker Street to assist Mr. Holmes in one of his mysteries?"

"I wish that were true," I returned, "but we're actually between cases at the moment."

"Ah, pity. Then perhaps I could interest you in a stroll out into a foggy London evening? See what kind of trouble we can find?"

"Bernard!" I exclaimed, surprised to receive such a proposition from a member of one of the most acclaimed families in England. "Are you quite serious?"

"Completely," he answered. "I'm afraid excursions into the unknown run in the bloodline. Can't be helped. And please, do call me Bernie. What do you say?"

Faced with such a charming invitation and the prospect of not much of interest going on back in Baker Street, I nodded my enthusiastic acceptance, and a few minutes later Bernie and I were in a cab rattling down cobblestone streets towards sections of London quite far removed from the staid and scholarly crowd of the Royal Society. It was the time of night when the decent, respectable side of London closes up its drapes and doors, and a quite different side of the city comes to life.

To get ourselves in the proper mood for whatever might come our way, our first stops were a couple of pubs, where I was much impressed with Bernie's familiarity with the area and the clientele. Things got progressively hazy after that, although I recall one conversation with a man who could pull his lower lip over his nose, and being cornered by a well-endowed matron who insisted that she was actually Persephone, Queen of the Underworld, and would I like a tour of her kingdom.

As a writer, my interest was quite naturally piqued at such an intriguing offer, but as a man of some experience, I made sure that my wallet was secure as I sidled away with a regretful shake of my head. At any rate, my overall sense of the evening was having a rattling good time with Bernie by my side. Yes, there is a somewhat disreputable side of London, but if you can swirl on the outskirts of it without being drawn into the vortex, there are a great many interesting things to be done and observed. Humanity at its best and worst unfolds in a kaleidoscope of tastes, smells, and sights. The most astonishing thing was how time seemed to speed up and then slow down, so that at one moment Bernie and I had sworn our determination to depart for the Galapagos Islands with a barmaid named Agnes the very next morning, and the next moment I was disconcerted to find myself standing alone at the bottom of our stairs at 221B.

Looking upward, to my dismay, I could see that the stairs were weaving in a steady, sinuous motion, and the prospect of getting up them in one piece was a daunting one. Getting a grip of the handrail, the popular tune from America, "Give My Regards to Broadway," popped into my head, and it was by singing this and focusing on the task at hand that I was able to methodically make my way up the stairs and enter our rooms. And it was then, to my utter astonishment, that I found both Holmes and Miss Adler looking at me in surprise.

"Good Lord!" I exclaimed. "You're still up!"

Holmes' eyes narrowed. "Watson, it's eight o'clock in the morning."

Looking out the window I could see that it was, in fact, daylight, a detail that appeared to have eluded me only moments earlier when I must have been dropped off at our rooms. A quick check of my pocket watch confirmed the time.

"Well, well, well..." I heard myself saying, for lack of anything better to say.

"We thought you were still asleep in your room," said Miss Adler. "Have you been out all night?"

"Apparently," I answered. "And now it's morning! Isn't that remarkable? The way the sun goes around the earth like that...day after day. Astonishing."

"Actually," Miss Adler corrected me, "if Mr. Copernicus is to be believed, it's the earth that revolves around the sun, I believe."

"Well, what's the difference, eh?" I responded, dimly aware that there was a massive difference, but not caring enough to worry about it at the moment, as my biggest concern was the peculiar way Holmes and Miss Adler were looking at me. I therefore felt that it was my duty to set their minds at ease.

"I'm not drunk, if that's what you're thinking. Not a bit of it."

"Weren't you going to some talk at the Royal Society last night?" enquired Miss Adler.

"Yes! Precisely! Francis Darwin! Talking about his father Charles and evolution and whatnot. And do you know who I found myself sitting next to? Bernard Darwin! Charles' grandson. Charming fellow! Superb golfer, apparently. Oh, and you'll never guess! Bernie Darwin is a Sherlock Holmes fan! He's read all of my stories in 'The Strand Magazine' and he was absolutely delighted to meet me. So, we went out. Bernie and I."

"Out where?" asked Miss Adler.

"Oh...here and there. Things have been a bit quiet around here lately, and I fancied a bit of adventure."

Miss Adler leaned forward, keenly interested. "And did you find it?"

"Miss Adler, there are some parts of London, you turn a corner, find yourself walking down a dark alley, you hear some kind of mysterious noise up ahead, and the hairs on the back of your neck stand straight up. God, I miss that feeling!"

"Where did you go exactly?"

I started to reply, but thankfully the cotton wool in my brains had started to clear just a bit. "Oh no. Nicely played, but you won't catch me out that easily. I went where I went, did what I did, and I'm not saying another word!"

Holmes approached me, looking me up and down in that disconcerting fashion of his, then took hold of my jacket lapel and sniffed it. His eyebrows arched upward as he turned to Miss Adler. "Opium."

"Dr. Watson! You spent the night in an opium den?" Miss Adler appeared to be quite surprised at Holmes' deduction, and I have to admit I was a bit surprised myself.

"No!" I answered. "Well, not all night. And don't you two get on your high horses with me! Ask Holmes about all the times I had to drag him out of some filthy drug den or another."

"On cases!" Holmes fairly shouted.

"Oh, we had some fine dust-ups together! Remember that night at the Bar of Gold in Swandam Lane? There must have been a dozen of them, wharf rats from the vilest corners of London, tattooed head to foot, but we sorted them out, didn't we Holmes? You should have seen him, Miss Adler! The finest exhibition of boxing and baritsu I have ever seen in my life! There wasn't a man he couldn't drink under the table or a scrape he couldn't get out of. My God, those were the days!"

I'm not entirely sure what kind of response I expected from Holmes as I reminisced about the halcyon days of our early cases, but it certainly wasn't what came out of his mouth next.

"My coddled eggs!" he exclaimed in alarm, and then he was out of the room and clattering down the stairs in a rush. I turned to Miss Adler, not quite certain that I had heard Holmes correctly.

"Is that a clue of some kind?" I asked.

"No, it's breakfast," she explained. "But sit down! Tell me more about your evening!"

"I'm not sure I can," I returned.

"Oh really? Does that mean that some sort of criminal activity was involved?"

"It means that copious amounts of various dubious substances were ingested more rapidly than good sense would indicate, and that I can't recall much in terms of our escapades, save for the fact that I was invited for a tour of the underworld by a large woman claiming to be Persephone, the daughter of Zeus and Demeter."

Miss Adler pursed her lips and gave a small shake of her head.

"You're disappointed in me," I said.

"I should say so!" she answered.

"I'm sorry."

"Don't be sorry! Take me with you next time, for God's sake!"

It was at this juncture that Holmes reappeared, wearing an apron over his robe, and carrying a tray with a covered dish.

"Here we are, my love!" Holmes uncovered the dish. "Coddled eggs, crisp bacon, lightly buttered toast, and a small fruit cup!"

Highly pleased with himself, Holmes backed up a step or two to better observe Miss Adler enjoying her breakfast. However, instead of diving right in, she contented herself with popping a grape from the fruit cup onto her plate, and then idly shuttling it back and forth between the coddled eggs using her spoon.

"It looks wonderful," she began, "but as Dr. Watson and I were talking, it occurred to me, have you given any thought to the crisis at the Foreign Office?"

"The what?"

"The Foreign Office case. We had the Foreign Secretary and his Under-Secretary here only yesterday. They're terrified that Germany is about to get their hands on some kind of new super-weapon."

"An exaggeration, I'm sure," replied Holmes. "Try the eggs."

"What about the Abernathy murder? It's not every day that a chimney sweep is poisoned with hemlock."

"Lovers' quarrel, probably. Shall I freshen your tea?"

"Lady Bracknell's lost puppy? The poor thing was in here sobbing her eyes out."

"With the size of her estate, it could be anywhere. Are you not hungry?"

Miss Adler put her spoon down with a sigh and looked at Holmes. "We need to talk."

At this, I discreetly pulled out my notebook and pencil, as something interesting was definitely in the wind, even if Holmes seemed to be clueless regarding the direction the wind was blowing.

"About what?" asked Holmes.

"Well, there is no gentle way to put this," returned Miss Adler, "so I'm just going to say it."

"By all means."

"Look at you."

"What?"

"You're wearing an apron and you're more concerned about coddled eggs and lightly buttered toast than any of those cases!"

"I'm not sure I follow."

"When I first met you," continued Miss Adler, "you were not the type of man who prepared fruit cups. You were an arrogant, self-absorbed drug addict, prone to depressive fits, and contemptuous of the police, women, and humanity in general. Your only redeeming quality was that you were easily the most brilliant and fascinating man I had ever met in my life. As was once remarked of the poet Byron, you were 'mad and bad and dangerous to know.'"

"Well, you were not exactly a paragon of virtue yourself, my dear. You were blackmailing the King of Bohemia and generally regarded as an adventuress of the worst kind."

"Guilty as charged. But then we fell in love, and now look at us." Miss Adler popped the grape into her mouth and fixed Holmes with a steady stare. "I want my Sherlock back."

Just as I was wondering how on earth Holmes would reply to this rather pointed criticism, a strong gust of wind rattled our windows and gave Holmes an excuse to look outside. With his hands behind his back, bouncing slightly on his toes, Holmes gazed out on Baker Street and I knew quite well that he was pondering what Miss Adler had just said and composing his reply. As for myself, I'm afraid that my attention drifted to the tray containing Miss Adler's breakfast, a fact that she picked up on immediately.

"Dr. Watson, I'm not overly hungry at the moment. Would you care for some coddled eggs and toast?"

"Are you quite sure?"

"Quite."

"Wonderful! I'm absolutely famished!"

"Well, you had a long night."

"That I did," I confirmed, making my way with the tray to the breakfast table. "Oh! And here's something I learned! After all his travels around the world, do you know what Charles Darwin's favourite dish was? Roasted guinea pig! Bernie told me that. And it reminded me of the Giant Rat of Sumatra. Remember that case, Holmes? Bit terrifying at the time, but now I'm wondering what Giant Sumatran Rat would taste like."

"That must have been before my time," said Miss Adler. "Did you ever write that story up?"

"No, I can't say that I did," I answered, scooping egg onto the toast. "There really wasn't a proper villain to make the story interesting. Mind you, we've had a number of cases like that. Remember the Repulsive Story of the Red Leech, Holmes? I thought we were done for that time."

"It sounds absolutely fascinating!" enthused Miss Adler, before turning to Holmes. "Do you remember those cases, dear? Back in the day when you actually took cases."

At this, Holmes turned from the window, and the dark look on his face encouraged me to focus my attention on the quite delicious fruit cup.

"That's unworthy of you, my dear," he remarked to Miss Adler. "And I know quite well what you're suggesting, but you're mistaken. I haven't changed. Not one bit."

Wordlessly, Miss Adler gestured at Holmes' apron, prompting him to remove it and fling it over the back of the divan.

"There is nothing wrong with wishing to keep one's robe unsoiled!" The effect of hearing himself utter those words was quite remarkable, and a look of astonishment spread over his face. "Good God...did I just say that?"

By way of comforting him, Miss Adler took Holmes by both hands and they stood for a long moment looking at one another.

"I have changed," said Holmes.

"We both have," agreed Miss Adler.

"What the devil happened?"

"We fell in love, with the result that we've both gone soft. And speaking for myself, I don't like it one bit."

"What do you think we should do?" asked Holmes.

"I'll tell you exactly what we're going to do," answered Miss Adler. "Whoever rings our bell next, we're taking the case. I don't care if there's a homicidal maniac loose in Stratford or if the Archbishop of Canterbury has misplaced his handkerchief, we're taking the case."

"Well, that's a rather broad spectrum. Perhaps if we—"

"We're taking the case."

"But—"

"We're taking the case."

"Fine." Holmes finally gave way to her insistence. "We're taking the case."

And with that, as it had so many times in the past at just such a propitious moment, our bell rang to announce the arrival of a visitor.

"Well, well, well," said Miss Adler with a smile. "It seems as if the gods were listening. I'll get it."

"I'm going to regret this," muttered Holmes as he slouched onto the divan.

Miss Adler turned at the door. "Oh, no you don't! Official Sherlock Holmes position, please!"

"For God's sake, Irene!"

"Clients have expectations. Now either you're Sherlock Holmes or you're not. What's it going to be?"

Like a sulky toddler, Holmes pulled himself off the divan and made his way to his armchair, whereupon Miss Adler took herself down the stairs to greet our visitor. Still working on the quite delicious coddled eggs, it was a painful thing for me to witness Holmes trying to get into character, as it were. He crossed his legs and immediately a grimace of concern appeared.

"No, Holmes," I offered. "You cross your right leg over your left leg."

"Ah! So I do," replied Holmes, reversing his legs and getting more comfortable.

"And you need a pipe."

"Of course!" Holmes sprang up and moved to the mantelpiece, his hand hovering over his selection of pipes. "What do you think, Watson? Briar, clay, or cherry-wood?"

"Definitely briar."

"Excellent!" Holmes put the briar in his mouth, sat down, then began the difficult task of deciding what to do with his hands. Putting them behind his head, he quickly realised that didn't feel right, then folded his arms across his chest before darting a quick glance in my direction. Polishing off the last bit of bacon, I steepled my fingers together by way of example, and with a look of recognition and gratitude, Holmes mimicked my pose just as our door opened and Miss Adler escorted our visitor into the room.

Dedicated readers of my modest efforts to recount the cases of Sherlock Holmes will remember that we have had all manner of entrances into our rooms over the years, ranging from the dramatic invasion of the enraged Dr. Grimesby Roylott to the spidery spectre of Professor Moriarty slowly ascending our staircase. In these more recent tales that I am now recording for posterity, including "The Adventure of the Elusive Ear" and "The Adventure of the Fallen Soufflé," there is no question whatsoever that I will always remember the first appearances of the bloodied Vincent Van Gogh, the dandy Oscar Wilde, and Bertie, the Prince of Wales for as long as I live, not to mention the cleaver-waving arrival of celebrated chef Auguste Escoffier. The gentleman now standing just inside our door was of a similar, highly striking disposition.

Chapter Two
The First Secret Invention

Tall, thin, and elegantly dressed, he wore a Prince Albert coat and a four-in-hand tie, with a white silk shirt, green suede high-top boots, and kidskin gloves. With his dark, wavy hair parted down the middle and a precisely trimmed moustache, his erect posture was complemented by his brisk, precise movements, and in his arms he carried a long, rectangular wooden case. Above and beyond all that were the man's striking blue eyes which, to borrow a term from the English philosopher Jeremy Bentham, seemed to form a veritable panopticon as his sweeping gaze took in the room. In other words, he positively radiated an all-seeing, all-knowing intelligence, the likes of which I had never experienced before, and I say that as a man quite familiar with not only Sherlock Holmes, but his brilliant brother, Mycroft, as well.

As Holmes stood up to greet the man, he extended his hand, but our visitor dismissed the offered handshake with a small shake of his head.

"You should really do something about those stairs," he commented in what I immediately recognised as an Eastern European accent.

"I wasn't aware there was a problem," answered Holmes.

"There are seventeen. Eighteen would be much better. Or perhaps fifteen. I prefer numbers that are divisible by three. I take it that you are Mr. Sherlock Holmes."

"Yes. And whom do I have the pleasure of addressing?"

"My name is Tesla. Nikola Tesla."

"The esteemed scientist and inventor?"

"The same. I come to you in the most dire circumstances imaginable. I have been robbed."

Upon hearing our visitor's name, I quickly finished the last piece of toast and brought out my notebook. Over the years I had heard and read about the mysterious Nikola Tesla and his many experiments with electricity. Much of it scarcely seemed credible, and yet there was no question that he was a man of unsurpassed genius, existing somewhere between myth and legend. To now see him in the flesh was a little overwhelming, and I could see that even Holmes was a bit overawed, because if there was one thing that Holmes could count on in almost any situation, it was being the smartest person in the room. The arrival of Tesla had changed that equation entirely. Still, the fact that he had been robbed and had come to Baker Street for help put Holmes on a little more even footing with Tesla than he would have been otherwise.

"Your reputation precedes you, Mr. Tesla, and I am very sorry to hear that you have been the victim of a crime," began Holmes. "I will, of course, be happy to consider your case. Please sit down and tell us all about it."

"May I get you some tea, Mr. Tesla?" offered Miss Adler as Tesla made his way to the divan.

"You are very kind. Yes, please." At this, Tesla paused to look at Miss Adler more closely. "Why...it is Miss Irene Adler, the American contralto, is it not?"

Holmes' eyebrows fairly leapt halfway up his forehead. "You two know one another?"

"We met once," continued Tesla. "At the Chicago World's Fair. August 17th, 1893." As he observed Miss Adler more closely, I saw Tesla flinch and avert his eyes. "If you would be so kind as to remove your earrings, I would be most grateful. I have a violent aversion to pearls."

"Of course."

As Miss Adler took off her earrings, I saw a wild, fearful look flash across Tesla's face.

"You don't have any peaches around here, do you?"

"Not that I'm aware," answered Holmes.

"Thank God for that," said Tesla with a shudder. "I find peach fuzz most unsettling."

I jotted down all of these peculiar details as quickly as I could. The articles I had read on Tesla focused largely on his patents and inventions, but had failed to mention his more eccentric side, which appeared to be quite considerable. Holmes eyed our visitor in what I must say appeared to be a somewhat wary fashion, the knowledge that Miss Adler and Tesla were already acquainted having clearly discombobulated him to a certain extent.

"Miss Adler must have made quite an impression for you to remember the exact date you met her," said Holmes.

"Indeed she did. In fact, I made a point of seeing her wonderful performance in Verdi's great tragic opera, 'Il Trovatore,' that very evening. But I also have a photographic memory."

At this, I'm afraid I rolled my eyes. "Oh, come now. I've heard people say that, but it's a lot of nonsense. Photographic memory my—"

"Watson!" interrupted Holmes. "A little decorum, if you don't mind."

Tesla didn't appear to be at all perturbed at my casting aspersions on the capabilities of his memory, and instead regarded me the way an entomologist might look at a beetle before pinning it to a board, that is to say, with a kind of clinical curiosity. Seeing a book on the side table next to him, Tesla picked it up and looked at the cover.

"Ah, 'The Awakening.' I have heard that it is a remarkable novel by a remarkable woman."

"Yes, it is," agreed Miss Adler, who had only begun reading it yesterday. "Unfortunately, it was so remarkable that it ruined Kate Chopin's career because she wrote about a woman who didn't simply aspire to being a wife and mother, but wanted her own life away from the world of men. She never published another book and died last year."

"A pity," said Tesla. "As the Serbian proverb says, 'A thorn pierces young skin more easily than old.'"

With that, he opened the book, scanned the first page, then handed the book to me and tapped the page with his finger. As I looked down at the print, Tesla gazed off into the distance and began reciting:

> "A green and yellow parrot, which hung in a cage outside the door, kept repeating over and over: '*Allez-vous-en! Allez-vous en! Sapristi!* That's all right!' He could speak a little Spanish, and also a language which nobody understood, unless it was the mocking-bird that hung on the other side of the door, whistling his fluty notes out upon the breeze with maddening persistence."

As Tesla spoke, I felt my blood run cold. He had only glanced at the first page for a moment, and yet...I looked up at Holmes and Miss Adler.

"Good Lord. That's word perfect."

"And with an excellent French accent too," added Miss Adler.

"*Merci beaucoup! Vielen Dank! Grazie mille! Nagyon szépen köszönjük!*" Tesla turned to me, and observing my open-mouthed reaction, continued, "I speak French, German, Italian, and Hungarian, along with Serbian and a few other Slavic languages."

"Remarkable," I managed. "If I might so bold as to enquire, what university did you attend?"

"I never graduated from any university," answered Tesla. "I do not do well in academic or business settings. I am self-educated, and have read Goethe, Descartes, Spencer, Shakespeare, Newton's 'Principia,' the novels of Paul de Kock, all one hundred volumes of Voltaire, and so on."

I turned from Tesla to Miss Adler. "How...how..."

"Did we meet? I attended Mr. Tesla's exhibition on electricity at the Chicago World's Fair. It was the most remarkable thing I have ever seen in my life. He held light bulbs in his hands and they lit up by themselves—"

"A simple demonstration of the wireless transmission of energy..." added Tesla.

"—then he took hold of two electrodes and was completely engulfed in the white fire of over two hundred thousand volts of electricity, sparks shooting off his body and clothing, but he was totally unharmed. I simply had to introduce myself when the performance was over."

Relieved that we seemed to be returning to more human territory, or at least territory that I understood, I let out a small laugh.

"Oh, I see. And then Mr. Tesla just happened to pop by your opera performance that evening. Now I understand why he remembers you so well."

"What is that supposed to mean?" asked Miss Adler.

"Nothing!"

"Are you suggesting that I slept with Tesla?"

Of course, that's precisely what I was suggesting because it made perfect sense. Two remarkable people meet one another, are instantly attracted, and then what happens happens. Still, I hadn't expected Miss Adler to question me directly on my meaning, and now had to find some way to gracefully extricate myself from the quicksand of my own presumption. Happily enough, before I had to do that, I saw Tesla waving his hand in the air.

"No, no, no! Excuse me, but that would be impossible. I would never do such a thing with Miss Adler. Or any woman."

"So you're a homosexual?" asked Holmes.

"Not at all," answered Tesla. "I prefer to remain celibate. I work at least eighteen hours a day and must preserve my energy, much as Isaac Newton and Leonardo da Vinci preserved theirs. Electricity is my mistress."

"But surely, you're a very handsome, brilliant, and successful man," I said. "Women must—"

"Yes, they do, but I refuse their advances. An inventor has so intense a nature with so much in it of a wild, passionate quality, that in giving myself to a woman I might love, I would give everything, and so take everything from my art...and it is a pity, for sometimes I feel so lonely. But then I remember, that other things being equal, the single man can always excel the married man. I hasten to add that I have also given up gambling, smoking, and coffee to better focus on my one true love, the subtle, vivifying fluid of electricity."

I'm afraid that at that juncture, Holmes, Miss Adler, and I found ourselves staring at this alien creature in our midst. It was Miss Adler who finally broke the spell in the most English way possible.

"I'll just get you that tea."

As Tesla took a seat on the divan and Holmes returned to his armchair, I stood at the ready with my open notebook, alert for whatever astonishing thing Tesla might say or do next.

"Needless to say," began Holmes, "I am delighted to make the acquaintance of such a remarkable man as yourself. Now then, down to business. What has gone missing?"

"A prototype," answered Tesla.

"Prototype of what?"

"I am afraid I cannot tell you."

"I'm sorry?"

"All I can say is that the loss is incalculable...it could lead to the end of civilisation...the end of humanity itself."

Holmes leaned back, clearly running this brief conversation through his head and endeavouring to make sense of it.

"So, let me make certain that I understand you correctly, Mr. Tesla. You want me to find something without knowing what it is?"

As Miss Adler set a cup of tea before him, Tesla held out the box he had brought with him towards Holmes.

"I brought you this."

Holmes took the box and opened it as Miss Adler and I crowded around to see its contents, while Tesla regarded us with perfect equanimity as he sipped his tea. Holmes glanced at Miss Adler and I before returning his attention to Tesla.

"It's an empty box."

"Of course it is empty," returned Tesla with perfect logic. "As I said, the contents have been stolen."

"Mr. Tesla..." Holmes seemed to be at a loss for words. "I'm sorry, but this won't do. You can't reasonably expect me to find—"

A forceful clearing of Miss Adler's throat drew Holmes' attention to her as she beamed her most beatific smile.

"You promised."

Exasperated by the situation, but feeling compelled to honour his pledge to Miss Adler, Holmes made a half-hearted attempt to get a bit more information out of Tesla.

"Very well. Can you give me a clue as to what was in the box? A hint, perhaps? Animal, vegetable, or mineral?"

"Even if I told you, you would not believe me." Tesla checked his pocket watch. "And now, if you will excuse me, I have an appointment regarding some funding that I desperately need. I will, of course, be back here for our appointment at 7:20 p.m." Tesla handed Holmes a card. "In the meantime, should it be necessary, I can be reached at The Savoy Hotel. Room 618. My thanks."

Finishing the remainder of his tea, Tesla stood up, bowed, then made his way to the door and exited, leaving his box behind and the door open. Struck by a moment of inspiration, I did a quick calculation in my notebook.

"Did you notice that, Holmes? Both Tesla's room number and the time of his appointment are divisible by three!"

"Yes," concurred Holmes. "Mr. Tesla does appear to be a man with some, shall we say, idiosyncratic tendencies. But perhaps you could help solve a mystery for me, Watson."

"Really? I'd be happy to!"

"Why in God's name are you making appointments without telling me?"

"But I didn't!"

Holmes looked to Miss Adler, who simply shook her head. "Well now, that is very odd indeed."

Picking up the box, I ran my eyes over it. "I say, Holmes, this is a bit of a puzzle, eh?"

With Tesla out of the room, Holmes could finally vent his frustration. "It's not a puzzle! It's absolutely asinine! How on earth can I be expected to find something when I don't even know what I'm looking for?"

"Sherlock Holmes could find it," interrupted Miss Adler. "At least, once upon a time..."

This brought Holmes up short. He would have been quite willing to abandon any attempt to find Tesla's missing item, but the same could not be said of disappointing Miss Adler. Taking a steadying breath, he turned to me.

"Watson, please be so kind as to fetch my magnifying lens."

As I moved to retrieve Holmes' lens, he picked up the box and regarded it closely.

"Very well, presumably the dimensions of this box give us a rough idea of the size of the object in question. It is clearly a tube or elongated object of some kind. Mr. Tesla referred to it in the singular, so it's reasonable to assume that there is only one item missing. Ah, here we are! A bit of cloth..."

Holmes pulled a small piece of fabric from the case just as I handed him his lens. I felt a small thrill of excitement run through me as Holmes sniffed the fabric and then held his lens up to it. This was like the old days. Somehow, this apparently innocuous clue would give Holmes the end of a thread, and through rigorous deduction and further investigation, he would follow that thread to its logical end and then, as if by some miracle, produce whatever it was that had been stolen from Tesla. As the seconds passed, I could barely hold in my anticipation.

"Well?" I asked.

"Well what?" Holmes answered, turning the piece of cloth in his fingers.

"Is it a specially woven fabric whose pattern and thread count tell us its country and city of origin?"

"Not exactly..."

"Oh, the smell! Is it imbued with a slight scent of tar indicating that the cloth was waterproofed, which means it was recently transported by boat and we can discover the ship it arrived on by checking dock records? Brilliant, Holmes!"

Holmes lowered his lens and regarded me with no small degree of exasperation.

"No, it appears to be a simple piece of common fabric, probably used to wrap up whatever was in here."

"Oh. I could have told you that."

Gamely trying to keep us on track, Miss Adler chimed in, "Perhaps the most valuable clue is to whom this box belongs..." Holmes looked at her in mystification. "Tesla! Nikola Tesla. What do we know about him?"

"Excellent, my dear! Yes indeed, let's consult the good old Index. Watson, if you would be so kind."

Rushing to our shelves, I swiftly removed the thick volume labeled "T" and began leafing through it.

"Here we are! Nikola Tesla...Serbian inventor. Born 1856. Expelled from school for gambling, immigrated to the United States in 1884, inventor of the alternating current induction motor and the Tesla Polyphase System, which was used to power the Chicago World's Fair and the revolutionary hydroelectric plant at Niagara Falls. Also the inventor of radio and—hang on. Wasn't it that Italian fellow who invented radio...what's his name?"

"Guglielmo Marconi," answered Miss Adler.

"That's it!"

"Apparently not," said Holmes, "at least according to my brother Mycroft. Marconi, while both industrious and inventive in his own right, essentially stole Tesla's work and then claimed it as his own. Quite in keeping with my own experiences regarding human nature, apparently wholesale theft and appropriating other people's ideas is extremely common in the scientific community. Tesla is a notable exception in that regard."

I continued reading Tesla's fascinating biography, "Demonstrated a remote-controlled boat at Madison Square Garden in New York in 1898 and was engaged in the so-called War of the Currents with Thomas Edison. Briefly worked with Edison, but then quit to start his own electric company. Donated patents to the Westinghouse Corporation to help keep the company solvent..." I looked up at Holmes and Miss Adler. "That can't be right. No one simply gives patents away."

"No one but Tesla," answered Miss Adler. "He is a visionary who wants his work to benefit all of humanity even if there is no profit to him. That is his dream...free, unlimited power for every single person on earth, with his machines doing the hard labour of the fields and the factories to give people around the world easier lives."

"But practically every city on the planet is using electricity based on his patents!" I exclaimed. "The lights in this room and all of London are due to Tesla's inventions. By all rights, he should be one of the wealthiest men in the world!"

"Which he clearly is not," added Holmes, "thus explaining his presence in London seeking funding for his newest invention."

"From what I learned speaking to him in Chicago," said Miss Adler, "he is not beloved by the investing class because his inventions threaten any number of well-established industries. The last I heard he was working on the wireless transmission of energy without any electrical meters, so that it can be given away for free. No investor would have any interest in that."

"What caused his falling out with Edison, I wonder?" I asked.

"Well," offered Miss Adler, "Edison is known to be extremely competitive and a bit sticky-fingered with other people's patents."

"Oh, come now, I can't believe that!" I objected. "Thomas Edison? He's practically the most famous man on the planet! The greatest inventor of all time! Now there's a man I would love to meet some day!"

Hearing our downstairs door open, there was a rush of footsteps on the stairs and a moment later a wild-eyed, middle-aged man burst into the room carrying a large case. His hunted expression reminded me of the arrival of a frantic Auguste Escoffier in our rooms some years earlier, but in this instance our guest's arrival was not accompanied by shouts and police whistles in the street. His fear was palpable, but the cause of it was not yet apparent. As had so often been the case in the career of Sherlock Holmes, we were only witnessing the end product of a long series of events, and once our guest recovered himself, we would begin the process of unravelling the circumstances that had led him to us.

Chapter Three
The Second Secret Invention

My first impression of the man was not a positive one, for he had a somewhat rumpled appearance, wearing a black jacket, white shirt, no tie, and shoes that had seen better days. A thatch of white hair was carelessly swept over his beetling black eyebrows and intense blue-green eyes. Keeping hold of his case, he rushed to our window, a stooping, shuffling figure who reminded me strongly of one of the great apes. Still out of breath, he turned back to us.

"Mr. Sherlock Holmes?" he enquired in an American accent.

"Yes?"

"You must help me! I am being chased through London by a pack of money-mad scoundrels! If they manage to—"

Our guest's attention was suddenly drawn to a flickering light bulb in one of our wall sconces.

"Hold on. What the hell's wrong with that lamp?"

"No idea," answered Holmes. "It does that sometimes."

Our guest put down his case and regarded us as if he were looking at a trio of Neanderthals.

"For pity's sake, light bulbs don't just 'do that sometimes.' There is a reason. There is always a reason if you take the time to investigate. But no. People these days are too damned lazy to do anything!"

Nimble as a cat, our guest rushed to the wall, stood on a chair, and began examining the light.

"Excuse me," began Holmes. "Much as I appreciate your attention to our lighting fixture...you said that you are being pursued?"

"Yes! Clearly, their spy network has learned that I'm in London!"

"Whose spy network?" asked Miss Adler.

"My enemies, of course! Morgan is behind this! I know it! Him and his damned banking cronies!"

"J. P. Morgan?" enquired Holmes. "The New York banker and financier?"

"Of course!"

"And what is it they want?" I asked.

"The contents of that case! It is the first and only model of the single most valuable invention in the history of mankind! They will do everything to steal it from me! May I trust you to safeguard it, Mr. Holmes?"

"Well, yes, of course, but—"

"There we are!" Somehow, our guest had contrived to solve our flickering lamp issue. "No trouble at all. Just a loose wire."

Jumping down from the chair, he turned to me. "That will be five pounds."

"What? Five pounds? You were only up there thirty seconds!"

"With the experience of a lifetime." He held his hand out. "Five pounds."

"That's outrageous!"

"Outrageous? You just had your damned light bulb fixed by Thomas Edison himself!" As we all looked at one another in surprise, he appeared to take umbrage at our stunned silence. "The Wizard of Menlo Park? Inventor of the light bulb? Inventor of the movie camera? Inventor of wax paper? Hello? Any of that ring a bell? Five pounds. And that's a bargain."

I looked to Holmes for guidance, and at his nod, reached into my wallet and then handed Edison a crisp five-pound note.

"Excellent!" Edison kissed the bill before shoving it roughly into his trouser pocket. "I can always tell the importance of one of my inventions by the amount of money it brings in." Bringing out his pocket watch, he checked the time and headed back towards our door. "Now then, I must run. I have a meeting with some investors that I can't miss! Guard that case with your lives! I can be reached at The Langham Hotel, but rest assured, I will be back for our appointment at 7:20!"

Exiting at speed, Edison was out the door and down the stairs before any of us could say a word. Coming out of my stupor, I turned to Holmes.

"Good Lord. That was Thomas Edison!"

"Why does everyone but me know that I have appointments at 7:20?" asked Holmes.

Miss Adler was already looking over Edison's case. "The same time Tesla said he would be back as well."

"Well, that should be interesting," noted Holmes. "At the very least, I suspect we'll learn the reason for their falling out and animosity towards one another."

"Do you think Edison stole some of Tesla's work?" I asked.

"No idea," answered Holmes. "But all of those inventions he just listed? He didn't actually invent any of them."

"You're joking. He's…Holmes, he's Thomas Edison!"

"I am aware of that. What you appear to be unaware of, Watson, is that Mr. Edison's true genius lies in taking other people's inventions, improving them, and then putting his name on them."

"And there's the difference between Tesla and Edison," added Miss Adler. "Tesla wants to help humanity, even if he doesn't make a penny. Edison scarcely takes a breath without calculating the profit. But now to more important things. What's in his case?"

"Well, let's just have a look, shall we?" said Holmes as he picked the case up and set it on a table. Pressing his thumbs against two latches, Holmes pushed them this way and that, but with no effect.

"It's locked, Holmes!" I said, kicking myself even as the words came out of my mouth, because Holmes habitually preyed upon obvious remarks such as that the way a vulture tears at carrion.

"Indeed it is," returned Holmes, moving to a desk drawer and opening it. For a moment, I thought I was going to be spared a withering assessment of my mental acuity, but as Holmes rummaged through the drawer, he couldn't help himself. "Your opium binge appears to have honed your deductive faculties to a razor's edge, Watson. But a simple lock has never stopped me before."

Holmes held up his lock-picking set of tools and approached Edison's case. Of course, I wanted to see what was in the case as much as I anyone, but I was also mindful of the fact that while Edison had entrusted us with what he had declared to be the most valuable invention in the history of mankind, he had never given us permission to unlock the case.

"I say, Holmes, should you really be doing that? It was left to us in confidence by Thomas Edison himself...and he did say he would be back. We can simply ask him what's in it when he returns."

With one of his tools hovering over the case's lock, Holmes paused.

"I suppose it would be a violation of his privacy."

"I should say so," I agreed.

"I certainly wouldn't want other people breaking into a locked case of mine."

"Of course not."

For a moment, we appeared to be at an impasse, until Miss Adler's ringing tones assailed our ears.

"Are you kidding me? Are you seriously—open the damned case!"

"But Irene—"

"Sherlock Holmes only recognises the law when he sees fit! Sherlock Holmes does whatever it takes to unravel a mystery! Sherlock Holmes...is Sherlock bloody Holmes! Now for God's sake, start acting like it!"

"You don't think Watson has a good point?"

With Miss Adler's stare threatening to peel the wallpaper off the walls, Holmes rapidly reassessed the ethics of the situation.

"I'm opening it, I'm opening it!"

Holmes immediately went back to work, and a moment later the latches sprang open. He lifted the lid of the case, and as Miss Adler and I strained our necks to get a glimpse of its contents, Holmes removed two embroidered pillows, a heavy ashtray, and half a dozen nondescript books.

"Is one of these the invention?" I asked.

Holmes picked up one of the pillows and looked at it closely. "I feel fairly certain that books, pillows, and ashtrays have already been invented. No, I suspect that these items replaced whatever was in the case originally and were most likely grabbed at random from Edison's hotel room when the contents of the case were stolen. Clearly, the idea was to try and replicate the weight of whatever was in here, with the pillows being used to secure the books and ashtray in place."

"Which means that unlike Tesla, Edison isn't even aware that he has been robbed," added Miss Adler.

"So this puts both Mr. Tesla and Mr. Edison in the same orbit, as it were," concluded Holmes. "Two world-famous inventors who have just been relieved of a valuable invention, with both of them in London to meet with investors."

"But I don't understand," I said. "Why would Edison need money? He's the most successful inventor in history!"

"Yes," agreed Miss Adler, "which means that he has been systematically preyed upon by bankers and lawyers for years. The larger the game, the larger the parasites."

"But he started General Electric, for God's sake! It's one of the biggest companies in the world!"

"Started it, but was then 'Morganised,' as the expression goes."

"What does that mean?" I asked.

"It means," continued Miss Adler, "that J. P. Morgan and his associates conspire to force you out of your own company in their efforts to create a monopoly that they then control. It's a business practice at which the robber barons in America excel...men like Rockefeller, Carnegie, and John Jacob Astor."

I shook my head. "This is getting too complicated for me. Tesla, Edison, empty cases and boxes, mysterious inventions, corporate thievery...what do you make of it all, Holmes?"

Miss Adler and I turned to Holmes, expecting, as we always did, that he would see some glimmer of light when all that we could perceive was darkness. Instead, he merely shrugged his shoulders.

"No idea. It's a mystery."

And with that, the greatest detective the world has ever known sat down in his armchair, picked up a newspaper, and began reading. It was at that precise moment that I became aware of Miss Adler's forefinger tapping rhythmically on the back of the divan, and while I couldn't describe it in any kind of coherent terms, I was aware that the atmosphere in the room had become highly charged. It came to me in a rush that this was a room that I should leave and leave quickly.

"You know what I'm going to do?" I began, having no idea what I was going to say next. "I am going to…tidy up my dresser. My dresser which is in my bedroom…which is over there…and which I am going to give a jolly good tidying…so that it's tidy…"

If either Holmes or Miss Adler heard a single word I said, they gave no sign of it, and so as I sidled out of the room, I began to sing the first song that popped into my head to fill the awkward silence.

> "Give my regards to Broadway
> Remember me to Herald Square
> Tell all the gang at Forty-Second Street
> That I will soon be there…"

"I do wish you would stop singing that infernal song, Watson," said Holmes without looking up from his paper.

"But it's a real toe-tapper, Holmes! You don't like George M. Cohan?"

With both Holmes and Miss Adler pointedly ignoring me, I knew it was fruitless to wait for an answer, and so I made my way into my bedroom, closed the door loudly, and then did what I often did in these situations—dropped down to the keyhole so that I could see and hear everything. For a few moments, there was a frozen tableau, until Miss Adler walked purposefully towards Holmes and tore the newspaper out of his hands.

"It's a mystery?"

"Isn't it?" returned Holmes, gamely trying to pretend that he wasn't as distressed as Miss Adler was.

"You have to pull yourself together."

"Oh really? You want me to investigate Tesla's empty box and Edison's ashtray, do you?"

"Why are you acting this way?"

"Because I've changed! Isn't that right? Isn't that what you just said not half an hour ago? And you're right. I have changed. And I'll tell you something else. Thank God!"

"What do you mean by that?" Miss Adler may have begun this rather tense exchange frustrated by Holmes' apparent disinterest in the problems of Tesla and Edison, but now there was a genuine note of concern in her tone.

Holmes looked up at her, his face working to conceal the emotions threatening to overwhelm him. Finally, he stood up, walked to the window, and stood there looking out at Baker Street. Miss Adler, showing the good sense that I had come to expect from her, kept her peace, waiting for Holmes to work out whatever it was he wanted to say next. At length, he took a shuddering breath and began.

"Do you know the condition I was in when I first met you? It wasn't pretty. I was fine when I had a case, but the moment a case ended I was back on the cocaine to ease the boredom and the pain of simply being alive. I would lie on that divan for days without moving, the blackest depression seeping like a viscous fluid into every corner of my brain. It was not going to end well, of that I can assure you. But then along came the case memorably described by Dr. Watson as 'A Scandal in Bohemia.' I met you and it was as if the heavens opened. Do you know, I remember every detail of the first moment I saw you? Right-hand profile, sapphire blue dress, wine-red lipstick, your eyes flickering in my direction every moment you thought I wasn't looking. You could have driven a harpoon through me and I wouldn't have noticed. You were the most brilliant and the most beautiful woman I had ever seen in my life."

Holmes turned to look at Miss Adler, and I don't think I have ever seen such an expression of raw emotion on his face.

"I could almost feel the chemicals in my brain rearranging themselves into a new pattern to accommodate the vision of you standing before me. And then, to my complete astonishment, you returned my affection. It was a revelation, and when we were alone for the first time and you reached out to touch my cheek, it was like nothing I had ever experienced, like emerging out of a shadowy pit and being enveloped within the sun without being harmed in any way. For the first time in my life, I felt known. I felt loved. And best of all, you allowed me to love you. So yes, perhaps my focus has drifted somewhat. Perhaps I am not the relentless, single-minded detective I once was. But I'm happy. As wild, improbable, and impossible an idea as I once thought that was, I am happy. Because I have you."

Any anger or frustration that Miss Adler was feeling had evaporated in the face of Holmes' heartfelt declaration.

"Do you think I don't know that? Don't you know that even hearing your footsteps on the stairs still sets my heart racing? But you're Sherlock Holmes. You have a responsibility to society. People need you!"

"Well, of course they do," returned Holmes. "Isn't that the way of the world? People always need saving from their own ignorance or the greed and cruelty of others. Check your history books, my dear. How often do we allow ourselves to be controlled and manipulated by the worst of humanity, allow ourselves to be seduced by lies and the joy of persecuting people just a little bit different than ourselves? Human beings can always be pitted against one another. People, tribes, nations. Look at the men we celebrate as our heroes. Alexander... Napoleon...Genghis Khan, men whose entire skill set consisted of slaughtering other human beings as efficiently as possible.

"Those are the heroes of the history books, the paintings and statues our schoolchildren gaze up at with wide-eyed wonder in the museums. And the famous men who don't look upon humanity as a single throat to be cut are often no better. Look at the men you just mentioned, the American robber barons, who cheat the system with watered stock and market manipulation, and whose sole focus in life is to hoard every scrap of silver and gold for themselves while children starve to death in the streets."

This was worrisome—a side to Holmes that I had never seen before, and it was clear this was also new to Miss Adler.

"Why are you talking like this?" she asked.

"Because I have spent my life immersed in the dark side of humanity. That is the nature and purpose of my profession. To hold back anarchy. To restore order. To descend upon a crime, a mystery, and to enact justice and make everything as clear as day. I create the illusion that the world can be understood if only we observe it closely enough and reason logically from those observations. There is no room for chaos in Dr. Watson's stories. No room for chance or accident. He rarely includes the cases where I fail, or the cases that begin with a child's brains splattered on the wall by a drunken stepfather. His stories offer comfort and certainty, whereas I know all too well that the howling universe doesn't care whether we live or die."

Moving to the mantel above the fireplace, Holmes removed the jackknife from a stack of pinioned letters and then held them aloft.

"You see these letters? Every one is a cry for help. From practically every corner of the globe. And it's not as if those cries are diminishing as civilisation advances. On the contrary, they increase with every passing day." Holmes began flipping through the correspondence. "Murder...theft...fraud...extortion...forgery...and those are only the crimes that can be prosecuted. What of our esteemed industrialists who quite happily poison the world for their own profit? Would you dare eat a fish from the River Thames? Would you dare go out in a peasouper, the fog and smoke from the factories so thick you can barely breathe or see your hand in front of your face? We are seduced by the siren song of progress, but we are on a path to eradicating ourselves. And do you know who will be most grateful for that? Every other species on the planet. Because humanity is a plague. A pestilence. Destroying and poisoning one another and everything we touch."

Tossing the letters back on the mantel, Holmes picked up his cherry-wood pipe.

"As for me, I am happy. In my tiny little corner of London, here in 221B Baker Street, I am happy. I have my pipe, my chair, a little problem of some interest from time to time, and I have you. That's all I can hope for, because I know without question that this world is beyond redemption."

Crouched behind my bedroom door, I was almost in a state of shock to hear Holmes speaking like this. It wasn't as if he had lost his senses or that there wasn't truth in everything he had said, but this was Sherlock Holmes, the last great refuge of lost causes and impossible cases. From my vantage point, I could see that Miss Adler was utterly taken aback as well.

"Oh my God. It's me," she finally managed. "I've done this. It's like Dr. Watson once said, 'Heroes don't have women in their lives.'"

"Wise fellow, that Watson," said Holmes. "Much wiser than he lets on in his stories, to be sure. He habitually plays down his own insights and contributions to our cases so that I might shine even brighter by comparison. Apparently, that's what his readers seem to want."

Pleased as I would normally be to hear such praise from Holmes, in the present situation it didn't do much to assuage the sick feeling in my insides. At a loss, Miss Adler threw her hands into the air.

"So, what do you want to do? Retire right now? Move to Sussex Downs and raise bees? Isn't that the plan?"

"That's not a bad idea at all," answered Holmes. "Should we start packing?"

At that, an expression crossed Miss Adler's face that I had never seen before and hope to never see again. With one step she moved towards Holmes and slapped him hard across the face. And as Holmes staggered backwards under the force of the blow, she caught him by his lapels and then kissed him on the lips just as hard, before quite literally flinging him into his armchair. Standing in front of him with her hands on her hips, cold fury poured out of her.

"Now you listen to me. You need to be better than this. You have to be. And no, this is not a discussion. What if the Foreign Office is right about Germany pursuing a new super-weapon and they get it and decide to start a war? What if the Abernathy murder isn't just a domestic case, but the next Lambeth Poisoner getting warmed up? And what if both of those could be prevented if you weren't sitting here twiddling your thumbs and making coddled eggs! Now, our priority at the moment is the inventions of Tesla and Edison, whatever they are. So, I am going to call Dr. Watson back in here. I am going to tell him to get his notebook out. We are going to go over the facts of the case, and we are going to logically proceed where those facts take us. Understood?"

Not waiting for Holmes' response, she looked towards my bedroom door.

"Dr. Watson! Come here! We need you!"

Immediately opening my door to join them, I wasn't two steps back inside the room before Miss Adler barked out, "Notebook!"

As I pulled out my notebook and pencil, she turned back to Holmes.

"You just sit. Listen. And think. Dr. Watson and I will list what we know so far and you need to try and make sense of it. So, Fact Number One—both Tesla and Edison have new inventions which they claim can alter the course of history."

"Fact Number Two," I added, "they both arrived in London at the same time with prototypes of their inventions."

"Fact Number Three—they both need investors to develop these inventions."

"Fact Number Four—both prototypes have gone missing."

Miss Adler and I turned our attention back towards Holmes, hoping that he would see some kind of pattern to this information, but fearful that he wouldn't. Getting up from his chair, Holmes moved to the mantel, struck a match, and relit his pipe. Giving it a meditative puff or two, he allowed his gaze to follow the smoke towards the ceiling.

"Very well. It is, of course, blazingly apparent that these are not isolated or unrelated incidents. There is a pattern, but Tesla and Edison are unaware of the roles they are playing. They were both lured to London by the prospect of funding, but then kept apart in different hotels, presumably until the moment is propitious to bring them together, which will apparently happen at 7:20 p.m. in these very rooms. Their respective inventions, therefore, must be linked in some way. Clearly then, events are being choreographed by some unseen person or persons. There is a web being woven, a dark web with a deadly black widow spider at its very centre. Remind you of anyone?"

Miss Adler and I looked at one another and fairly shouted our response, "Marie Chartier!!!"

Chapter Four
The Government Agent

It was at that moment, precisely as if we had summoned a genie from a bottle, that Marie Chartier appeared at our open door. We had encountered the brilliant, beautiful, and unrepentantly wicked daughter of Professor Moriarty in two previous cases, "The Adventure of the Elusive Ear" and "The Adventure of the Fallen Soufflé," cases that I had been unable to write up for "The Strand Magazine" due to their sensitive nature and the eminent personalities involved. However, just as with this case, I had taken the trouble to set them down for posterity, and the manuscripts were currently resting quite comfortably in my old despatch box in care of Cox and Company.

"You called?" purred Miss Chartier in her French accent, the product of a childhood spent in Switzerland. As she glided further into the room like a panther, I was struck by her long, flowing dress, cinched tightly at the waist, and her green, intelligent eyes that missed nothing. Still, as impressive and compelling as her presence was, it ran a distant second to the two items she was carrying with her—cases identical to the cases left with us by Tesla and Edison.

"And so we meet again," she continued, "as I knew we would."

Glancing around the room, a small smile made its way to her face as she observed the portraits of Vincent Van Gogh and King Edward VII on our walls.

"I like to think I got the better of you in the case involving Van Gogh and Oscar Wilde, but I will admit that you bested me when I tried to take advantage of His Royal Highness and Auguste Escoffier. And so it comes down to this—our third and,

I would wager, final confrontation." She turned her attention to Miss Adler. "And what a pleasure to see you again, Miss Adler. Are you still pretending to be the housekeeper, Mrs. Hudson, since Dr. Watson so cruelly killed Irene Adler in the first Sherlock Holmes short story?"

In the early days of our Mrs. Hudson charade, Miss Adler had adopted a rather alarming Cockney accent for our supposed housekeeper, and seeing an opportunity to unleash it once again, she did not disappoint.

"Cor blimey, only when necessary, luv! You know how it is, people might not approve of Mr. Sherlock Holmes having his own cheese and kisses..."

"Oh, I know that one!" I said, pleased to have deciphered the infamous Cockney rhyming slang. "Cheese and kisses...his missus! Well done! I do love your Mrs. Hudson character!"

"It is quite a *tour de force*," agreed Miss Chartier. "Still, if Sherlock Holmes can die and come back to life, why not Irene Adler? A little resurrection never killed anyone."

"I'll take it under consideration," replied Miss Adler as Miss Chartier paused in front of the cases left behind by Tesla and Edison.

"Interesting. I see that you have made the acquaintance of Nikola Tesla and Thomas Edison."

"And I observe that you have brought with you cases identical to theirs, Miss Chartier," returned Holmes.

"Indeed. I can explain." Setting her cases down, Miss Chartier proceeded to sit quite delicately on the divan, her hands crossed in her lap, and looking every inch the innocent debutante. "I do not know what you must think of me, and it is true that in the past I may have conducted myself in a manner unbecoming for a lady. However, I am a changed woman, and you will be delighted to learn that I am now earning an honest living."

"You?" I'm afraid I couldn't keep the incredulity out of my voice. "Working for whom?"

With as much of a flair for drama as Holmes, Miss Chartier waited a moment, looking at each one of us in turn, before pronouncing, "The British government."

I couldn't stop the laugh that burst out of me. "The British government? That's ridiculous! Oh, let me guess! Did Prime Minister Balfour solicit your opinion on the Russo-Japanese War? Perhaps he required your expertise on British policy towards the mutiny on the battleship Potemkin a few months ago!"

"Perhaps," teased Miss Chartier. "I may have enjoyed a brief vacation in Odessa on the Black Sea."

"Oh, I don't believe a word of it!" I continued. "You're the daughter of Professor Moriarty and utterly steeped in evil! Brilliant, yes, but also scheming, conniving, and capable of just about any crime imaginable!"

If I expected any kind of retraction or admission of telling a tall tale from Miss Chartier, it was not forthcoming. Instead, she simply sat quietly, letting the weight of her extraordinary claim settle into us until Miss Adler observed, "The very qualities that every government requires from time to time…with a suitable amount of discretion, of course."

"Just so," agreed Miss Chartier.

At this, a look of both dread and realisation entered Holmes' eyes. "No, no. Don't tell me..."

"Oh, but I must tell you, Mr. Holmes," insisted Miss Chartier. "In fact, I have been positively aching and longing to tell you. You see, I was commissioned by a very high-ranking member of the British government to acquire two items. Let me see if I can recall the gentleman's name...oh yes, Mycroft Holmes."

"Mycroft!" I exclaimed. "Why, that's your brother, Holmes!"

"Don't remind me."

Of course, the mention of Mycroft Holmes changed everything. At this point in time, I had only met him once, in "The Adventure of the Greek Interpreter," and he was, to all appearances, simply a minor official in the vast bureaucracy of the British government, but as Holmes had confidentially informed me, there were occasions when Mycroft effectively *was* the British government. Running things quietly behind the scenes, Mycroft had a free hand to operate as he saw fit, and it was well within the realm of possibility that he would commission a woman of so many talents as Marie Chartier to do his dirty work.

"He is a most charming fellow," added Miss Chartier, "but then, almost anyone would be charming with the weight of the British Treasury behind them. He had heard of my small reputation, mentioned a very flattering number in pounds sterling, and thought I might be of use to him in procuring certain items."

"Fascinating," said Holmes. "Of course, your story is riddled with any number of fabrications, but fascinating fabrications nevertheless."

"I do not know what you mean," answered Miss Chartier.

"Then let me see if I can translate your fanciful little tale. I don't doubt for a moment that my brother Mycroft is involved, because that can be easily verified. However, would he hire you and put you on His Majesty's books for services rendered? No, I think not. What's more likely is that he has certain information concerning your criminal activities in England that would be extremely inconvenient for you were that information to be conveyed to Scotland Yard. He desires something from two non-British citizens, Edison and Tesla, so he contacts another non-British citizen—that would be you, Miss Chartier—to assist him using whatever leverage he has against you. That way both he and the British government are not directly involved and plausible deniability can be maintained. Is that, perhaps, closer to the truth of the matter?"

"Let us say that your brother is very persuasive and leave it at that," returned Miss Chartier.

"Gladly," agreed Holmes. "Now then, tell us more about these items belonging to Mr. Tesla and Mr. Edison that you have been commissioned to procure."

"It all began, as so many things do, with secret whispers," began Miss Chartier. "There were rumours about their latest inventions—rumours dismissed as fairy tales by most sensible people. The inventions were too incredible, too fantastic and bizarre. And yet, when talking about Tesla and Edison, it is not wise to make too many assumptions regarding what is and what is not possible. And so I lured both gentlemen here with the promise of English investors with private fortunes and open chequebooks, reserved rooms at The Savoy and The Langham to keep them apart because they do not like each other very much, and *voilà!* Here we are."

"Where are we, exactly?" I asked, most definitely intrigued by Miss Chartier's tale, but uncertain regarding what her story might portend.

"Nowhere," Miss Adler noted, "if Miss Chartier's cases are as empty as ours."

"An excellent point, Miss Adler," agreed Miss Chartier. "Happily, my cases are quite full. You see, once my contacts in America informed me that Tesla and Edison were booked for steamships headed for England, I simply asked for a full description of any luggage they personally brought on board with them, knowing that if it was a new invention they would scarcely take the chance of putting it into storage aboard the ship. Once they arrived in London and were checked into their hotels, it was a simple enough matter to take their cases and replace them with duplicates. The cases I brought with me have both been in the possession of the British government for the past two days and their contents have been examined by their very finest experts."

"And?" I could scarcely wait to hear what kind of wondrous inventions Tesla and Edison had come up with.

"And nothing, my dear Watson," said Holmes. "Miss Chartier would scarcely be here otherwise."

"Exactly right, Mr. Holmes," agreed Miss Chartier. "No one has any idea how they work, or if they work. They are quite the mystery. Which is why Mycroft suggested that I engage the services of his little brother...the great Sherlock Holmes."

"Of course," Holmes nodded. "Brilliant though he may be, Mycroft has always been plagued by congenital laziness. It's not the first time he's done this. So, let's see what you've brought us."

"*Bien!*" Miss Chartier flashed the dazzling smile that had led more than one unfortunate man to his doom. "Won't it be nice, Mr. Holmes, to finally work on the same side together?"

"It would be," agreed Holmes, "if I believed for one moment that were true. Let's begin with Mr. Tesla's invention."

With no undue fuss or fanfare, Miss Chartier opened Tesla's box and removed what appeared to be an elongated, futuristic-looking object of some kind.

"*Voilà!*"

"What in God's name is it?" I asked. "Is it a model of some kind?"

"No, this is the invention itself. Can you not guess its purpose?"

"I can guess." All eyes turned to Miss Adler as she took the device from Miss Chartier. "From the moment Tesla described its loss as possibly causing 'the end of humanity itself,' I had an inkling of what it might be," began Miss Adler. "And now, seeing it before me, and knowing what I know of mankind, I feel quite certain I know what it is. It is a weapon. Presumably a weapon of almost incalculable power."

"Bravo, Miss Adler!" Miss Chartier softly applauded. "It is indeed a very special weapon with a wonderfully evocative name. It is...a Death Ray."

"How do you know that?" I asked.

"Upon Tesla's arrival, we had a wonderful dinner and shared a bottle or two of champagne at The Savoy. He really is a very charming fellow and quite happy to discuss his work once he is in a more, shall we say, relaxed state of mind."

"And I don't doubt," began Holmes, "that once he had revealed its purpose to you, you poured him another glass of champagne and encouraged him to talk about it in intimate detail."

"You know me so well, Mr. Holmes," answered Miss Chartier. "Of course, that is exactly what I did." Taking the weapon back from Miss Adler, Miss Chartier turned it in her hands. "It is a charged particle-beam weapon, capable of producing one hundred thousand volts of electricity and killing anyone it touches. It is, quite simply, one of the most unique and deadly weapons ever created."

"And presumably," added Holmes, "the kind of weapon that the more militaristic European powers would be most interested in acquiring...Germany, for example."

"Oh, I would expect so, yes. Would you like to see it work?" Miss Chartier turned the Death Ray towards me and pointed it at my chest. Instinctively, I raised my hands.

"I don't think that's necessary!"

"Oh, I think it is. Anyone can claim to invent a Death Ray, and Tesla is famous for making all kinds of grandiose announcements and promises. How do you English put it? 'The proof is in the pudding?'"

"Miss Chartier, please!" Although I was aware that she had just told us that the finest British experts had failed to discover how to make the weapon function, the fact that it was pointed directly at me was still unnerving in the extreme, a fact that Miss Chartier clearly relished.

"Come now, Doctor. This is your chance to go down in history as the first victim of Tesla's Death Ray. I simply pull this trigger and..."

I heard the audible click of the trigger and clenched my teeth, waiting for my insides to be incinerated, but mercifully, the weapon didn't fire. Accentuating her point, Miss Chartier proceeded to pull the trigger a few more times, but with no result.

"...nothing," observed Miss Chartier. "It will not fire. The finest minds in England couldn't even turn it on. Their conclusion was that Tesla, as he often does, has exaggerated his accomplishment somewhat."

"Thank God for that!" I exclaimed as Miss Chartier returned the Death Ray to its box.

"And Edison's invention?" asked Miss Adler.

"See for yourself." Miss Chartier opened up Edison's case and removed a wooden box with a red light bulb protruding from the top of it. Looking at the box more closely, I observed that there was a lens embedded within it and some sort of switch on the side. Reaching into the case again, she pulled out a bizarre-looking orb of glass with what appeared to be two curved pieces of metal inside it. To all the world, it appeared to be nothing more than a random series of spare parts that Edison might have assembled in his workshop to amuse a small child.

"And this doesn't work either?" I asked.

"No," answered Miss Chartier. "Even worse, no one knows what it is or what it is supposed to do. Edison will not say a word about it, although for what it is worth, I do have my own thoughts on what it might be."

"Well, let's have a look," began Holmes. "It's in two parts, but two parts that don't appear to fit together or to be related to one another."

"Then let's separate them." Taking the glass orb with her, Miss Adler retreated to the far side of the room.

"I have it on good authority from the British experts that what you are holding, Miss Adler, is a photoelectric cell," remarked Miss Chartier. "We simply flip this switch on the side of the box and much like a movie projector, it sends a beam of light from this lens to the cell."

Miss Chartier flipped the switch on the box, but with no apparent effect.

"Nothing," I observed.

"Not to our eyes," answered Miss Chartier. "That is the one thing the British experts were actually able to discover. What is being emitted from the lens is an infrared beam of light powered by a small battery within the box."

"Ah," said Holmes, "then this box would also be a receiver of some kind. And presumably, if the infrared beam gets broken between the lens and the photoelectric cell, this red light goes on to alert the observer. Intriguing. But to what purpose?"

"Oh, I see!" I exclaimed. "Do you know what it is? Why, it's a burglar alarm! You have this inside your front door and if anyone enters your home and breaks the infrared beam of light, then some sort of lights or alarms will go off! It's quite brilliant!"

"An interesting theory, Watson, and in this instance, quite easy to verify." Holmes placed his hand in front of the lens, but the bulb atop the device remained dark.

"And there is your problem, Mr. Holmes," said Miss Chartier. "Two devices created by the greatest geniuses in the world, but neither one of them works."

"And what do you expect me to do?"

"Make them work. Scientists, locked within their little specialities, have their limitations, but you are a deductive genius...perhaps the only mind in the world to equal Tesla and Edison. If anyone can unravel how these devices work, it is you. Now, if you don't mind, I will just pour myself a glass of your most excellent sherry while I watch the greatest mind in England solve these two remarkable puzzles."

Thanks to her previous visits to our rooms, Miss Chartier was well acquainted with the location of our sherry decanter and made her way to it with unerring accuracy. As she opened the decanter, Miss Adler put in her request.

"Make that two sherries."

Feeling that I could use a large whisky or two myself, instead I took out my notebook and regarded Holmes with a mixture of hope and trepidation. True, he had been a bit off his game of late, but surely the combination of Tesla and Edison seeking his help would bring him back to his old self, especially now that we knew that both Mycroft Holmes and Marie Chartier were also involved. At the very least, I didn't want to see him humiliating himself in front of Miss Chartier, and so I held my breath as Holmes picked up Tesla's Death Ray and regarded it from all sides. Now knowing what it was, I found the device most intimidating. From a large rectangle of metal emerged smaller rectangles, both on top of and below the weapon, with a silver tube emerging from the front of it and a rudimentary stock at the back.

"Well..." began Holmes, "this would clearly be the barrel of the weapon, as it were...the place where the energy beam would presumably emerge...after being generated in this part back here. I'm afraid I'm not overly familiar with particle-beam weapons."

Holmes was turning the device over in his hands, clearly at sea. Looking over at Miss Chartier and Miss Adler, I observed that they both had their sherries, and that Miss Chartier was looking at Miss Adler with a quizzical expression as Miss Adler smiled in embarrassment.

"Perhaps Edison's device, dear?" offered Miss Adler hopefully.

"Yes, of course!" Discarding Tesla's Death Ray, Holmes picked up Edison's box and scrutinised it closely.

"It's...well, it's a wooden box. Pine, if I'm not mistaken. Hewn with a crosscut saw, I believe. Somewhat hastily fashioned...could use a bit more sanding to smooth down the edges, quite honestly. No one likes a splinter, am I right?"

As I felt my heart edging up to my throat, I heard Miss Chartier laugh.

"Most amusing, Mr. Holmes. Now seriously, what do you deduce, because I have my suspicions regarding Mr. Edison's device."

As Holmes hesitated, Miss Adler plucked Miss Chartier's sherry glass from her hand.

"No, I'm sorry! We're not doing this! Sherlock Holmes is not some show pony here for your amusement!"

"What do you mean?" objected Miss Chartier. "He likes showing off!"

"Not anymore! He only works in private!"

"I want to know how these work before Tesla and Edison get here!"

Miss Adler raised her eyebrows. "Of course. It was you who arranged that meeting."

"At the insistence of Mycroft Holmes," answered Miss Chartier. "He felt that their competitiveness and mutual dislike for one another might be useful."

"Well, I'm sure Holmes will have everything figured out by the time they arrive. Now please go."

"But I want to watch! And your sherry is most delicious."

"You need to leave." By way of emphasising her point, Miss Adler pulled out a sword from amongst our fireplace tools. "Now."

"Very well." Miss Chartier didn't appear to be unsettled at all by the sword at her throat. "I have no desire to cause a scene...at least not yet. But I shall be back with Tesla and Edison this evening."

Never one for long goodbyes, Miss Chartier was out the door and down the stairs a moment later, leaving Miss Adler and I to look at Holmes as he disconsolately put Edison's invention down and then slumped into his armchair. Coming up behind him, Miss Adler rubbed his shoulders and kissed him on the cheek.

"Never mind, darling. You know what? I'm making you nervous and you can't very well be expected to focus on your work when there's a gorgeous woman who adores you standing just a few feet away. So, I'm just going to run out to the Diogenes Club to have a word with your brother Mycroft regarding his arrangement with Miss Chartier, and perhaps do an errand or two. Dr. Watson? Can I interest you in a bit of fresh air?"

"No, I'm fine," I replied, only to immediately realise from Miss Adler's stare of disapproval that I had answered incorrectly. "Actually, that's a wonderful idea! Yes! A good stroll is just the thing! Let's clear the cobwebs, shall we? Holmes will have everything in order by the time we get back!"

Miss Adler and I made our way to the door, but she turned for one last word with Holmes. "Get yourself a fresh pipe and clear your mind. You can do this."

We paused, waiting for Holmes to do something or say anything, but he never moved nor spoke a word, and so we made our way down to the street. Standing outside of 221B, both Miss Adler and I were both clearly in some degree of distress. I knew this from the shuddering breaths she was taking, and no doubt she knew the same by the manner in which I was staring fixedly at a chimney some one hundred yards away and not daring to speak. At length, I felt her hand on my arm.

"Let's go see Mycroft."

Chapter Five
The First Secret Revealed

Fifty yards down Baker Street, I was about to make some kind of innocuous comment regarding the weather, when a thought occurred to me that stopped me in my tracks. Seeing this, Miss Adler came to a halt as well, looking at me questioningly.

"Miss Adler," I began, "I don't know that there's a polite or judicious way to put this, but they don't actually allow women in the Diogenes Club."

She reached out towards me, and her fingers were like iron bands across my forearm. "Well then, won't our visit be a pleasant surprise for everyone?"

What followed I shall fully relate in due course, but for the moment the only thing in the minds of Miss Adler and myself was the well-being of Sherlock Holmes. Indeed, as I had surmised, when we arrived at the Diogenes Club we were summarily informed that women were not welcome within their hallowed walls. This unwelcome news was delivered by a bushy-moustached octogenarian, whose curt, dismissive speech had doubtless been honed to a fine edge over the course of a few decades.

There was then a brief but rather memorable conference between Miss Adler and the gentlemen in question. As much as I would like to relate the actual words that were exchanged, I'm afraid I couldn't actually hear anything that Miss Adler said. Gripping the old fellow by the collar, she pulled him towards her and hissed a few short syllables into his ear, whereupon he speedily agreed to make an exception for her. As had often proved to be the case in our association with Miss Adler, her complete and utter disregard for convention and propriety had the charming effect of overwhelming many of the fossilised rituals of decorum that stunted so many aspects of British society.

After we were ushered into the Stranger's Room to wait for Mycroft, Miss Adler and I had a few minutes to ourselves to discuss the events of our rather remarkable morning. We agreed that there was little to be done regarding the mysterious inventions of Tesla and Edison, but the meeting at Baker Street later in the day would surely result in those matters being clarified to a considerable extent. Then there was the larger problem of Sherlock Holmes.

Every exemplar in every field has peaks and valleys in their career. This is true of composers, of athletes, and as I can attest, to writers as well. For example, proud as I am of many of my Sherlock Holmes stories, I must admit that my recounting of "The Adventure of the Stockbroker's Clerk" was simply a sad rehash of "The Red-Headed League," which I had published two years earlier. Holmes, Miss Adler and I agreed, had been in a downward spiral for some time now, with promising cases increasingly looked upon as inconveniences to be avoided if at all possible.

When the estimable Mycroft Holmes finally condescended to join us, he was much as I remembered him, moving lightly given his considerable bulk, and possessed of the same grey and penetrating eyes as his younger brother. We enquired as to his association with Marie Chartier, and with the well-practised evasiveness of a lifelong diplomat, he confirmed that she was working at his behest while never actually saying that directly. He too, was most anxious to learn more about the inventions of Tesla and Edison, but it was our revelations concerning the malaise of Holmes that gave him pause. He considered the problem for a full thirty seconds as Miss Adler and I sat in silence, before pronouncing, "That simply won't do." In this, we were all in agreement and it was some comfort to be in the company of the two people in the world just as concerned about Holmes as I was.

Given all we had to discuss, Mycroft rang for the porter to order refreshments. It was with some surprise that we learned that Mycroft was fully convinced that Edison's invention had something to do with long-range radio transmissions and he was terrified that the Germans would get hold of the technology before England. At this I kept my tongue, for while I could see the utilitarian advantages of such a scientific advance, it didn't seem consistent with Edison's extravagant claims, although perhaps that was merely the salesmanship side of Edison coming to the fore to help drive up the price.

As for Tesla's device, Mycroft knew that it was a Death Ray thanks to Miss Chartier's champagne-fuelled interrogation of Tesla at The Savoy. It appeared that either it didn't work, or Tesla's natural caution had led him to bring an incomplete prototype, but here Mycroft fixed Miss Adler and myself with a steady stare.

"It works," he began. "Given the specific details Tesla was able to provide regarding its capabilities, there is no question in my mind that he has tested it. It can be made fully functional the moment that Tesla wishes it to become functional. However, he has proved immune to both monetary and patriotic appeals, hence the idea of putting him in a room with Edison. Brilliant though both men may be, they are like a pair of professional beauties constantly seeking to outdo one another. Ego and jealousy are the tools we will use to pry open the secret to Tesla's Death Ray. You may depend upon it."

"That's all very well and good," said Miss Adler, "but in all candor I could care less about either Tesla's or Edison's inventions. What about Sherlock?"

It was some time later that Miss Adler and I found ourselves squinting in the late afternoon sun outside the Diogenes Club. As pedestrians scurried past us on their way home or perhaps out to dinner, Miss Adler looked at me and read my pained expression. "Headache?"

"Pounding," I affirmed, before adding, "I need a pint or two. Or three."

"Meet you back at Baker Street at 7:00?" she asked.

I nodded. "And do you think all of our guests will arrive on time?"

"I do," she answered. "Each for his or her own reasons. Make sure your pencil is sharpened, Doctor. I suspect that the events of the evening will provide you with the material for a most exceptional case."

And with that, Miss Adler and I went our separate ways. Happily enough, within two blocks I was able to find a pub that wasn't too crowded and served a most excellent glass of bitter. The events of the day and the prospects of the evening had unsettled my stomach to the extent that I couldn't really contemplate a full meal, but I did manage to enjoy a few Scotch eggs to help keep my strength up. As Miss Adler had indicated, an evening spent in the company of Thomas Edison, Nikola Tesla, and Marie Chartier was bound to result in the kind of material that I hadn't had at my disposal for some time. Holmes, I felt certain, would rise to the occasion, but I was aware that my loyalty to him coloured my expectations to a considerable degree.

Taking my notebook out, I ordered a second pint and began writing down everything that had transpired so far while the memories were fresh in my mind. I am always very particular about trying to quote people accurately, and so I proceeded to jot down everything I could remember regarding the earlier conversations with Tesla, Edison, and Miss Chartier. I then began to roughly order those conversational snippets into a rudimentary narrative. Given the potential stakes at play, I felt a bit cold-blooded and guilty doing this, but it was nothing more than my writerly instincts coming to the fore. When faced with the unknown or something I don't understand, I have found that the best way to explain it to myself is by writing a story.

By the time I put my notebook back into my pocket and ventured out of the pub, I calculated that I had just enough time to walk back to Baker Street and be there by 7:00. Normally, I enjoy walking through the streets of London and observing the sights, but now I was so preoccupied regarding recent events that I was back on Baker Street before I knew it. Just as I neared our front door, a cab stopped and Miss Adler emerged, right on time. She was almost unrecognisable, as while I had buried myself in a quiet corner of a pub, she had made the rounds of some of London's finest stores and was sporting a new hat, new dress, and new boots, all of which added to her normally striking and statuesque appearance. She pirouetted gracefully for my approval.

"What do you think?" she asked. "Will it bring Holmes out of his doldrums?"

"I have no idea," I answered, "but you've certainly brought me out of my doldrums."

Miss Adler laughed and pinched my cheek, then we paused before our front door as our levity rapidly disappeared, the same thought clouding our minds. Would Holmes be in? Was it possible that he had penetrated the secrets of Tesla's and Edison's inventions? And if he hadn't, what state of mind would he be in?

Arm in arm, Miss Adler and I made our way up the stairs. Whatever we found, for good or ill, we would share together. Opening the door to our rooms, we both entered and looked around. It was quiet, and even more disturbingly, there was no haze of thick smoke in the air as there normally was when Holmes was presented with, as he would put it, "a three-pipe problem."

Coming further into the room it was evident that Holmes wasn't there. His armchair was empty and he was not buried in some experiment in his chemical corner; in fact, our rooms were precisely as we had left them. But then, I spotted the single exception, and it was an exception that practically broke my heart the moment I laid eyes on it. It was Holmes' magnifying lens—snapped in two and with the glass shattered—laying in pieces on the floor. Carefully, I gathered up the broken remains and wordlessly held my hand out to Miss Adler. We both stared in disbelief, and then hot tears were streaming down both of our cheeks.

A moment later her arms were wrapped around me, just as mine were wrapped around her, and there we stood, clinging to one another like shipwreck survivors in the open sea. Although we had never said as much out loud, Holmes was the bedrock of our existence, and now that bedrock was gone.

"He needs our help," began Miss Adler haltingly. "We're his only friends in the world and we must do everything we can."

"I know," I managed to reply.

But before we could do anything or say another word, the downstairs door opened and what sounded like a herd of elephants began ascending the stairs. I instantly recognised the agitated voices of Tesla and Edison arguing.

"...I do not know what you are talking about!" Tesla was saying. "I did everything you asked me to do!"

"I'm not saying you didn't!" returned Edison.

"So you agree?"

"With what?"

At that, Tesla and Edison burst into our rooms, followed by a clearly exasperated Marie Chartier, who headed straight for our sideboard to pour herself a sherry. As for Miss Adler and myself, we did our best to compose ourselves as Tesla and Edison continued their squabbling.

"You still owe me fifty thousand dollars!" shouted Tesla.

"For God's sake, that was ages ago!" answered Edison.

"What difference does that make?"

"Because I can't even remember what you did!"

"Oh really?" Tesla was incredulous. "Well, happily enough, I happen to have an exceptional memory! And when you hired me in New York and I saw the primitive design of the dynamos at your Pearl Street power plant, I offered to improve them, and you agreed to pay me fifty thousand dollars for the job. I then redesigned twenty-four dynamos and also installed automatic controls for which patents were obtained. But did you pay me?"

"Did you really expect me to pay you fifty thousand dollars?"

"Why wouldn't I?"

"You know what your problem is Tesla?"

"No, apparently I do not!"

"You just don't understand the American sense of humour!"

Tesla turned away from Edison in disbelief and began cursing in what I believe was Serbian. "*Bog te jebo! Dabogda komsiji crkla krava!*"

"Speak English, Tesla!" yelled Edison. "You're in England!"

"Speak English?" Tesla came back towards Edison, his face red with emotion, and offered a rather explicit translation that I cannot repeat here verbatim. Suffice to say the first insult involved God committing an unnatural act upon Edison and the second expressed the fervent wish that the cow of Edison's neighbour would suffer an untimely demise.

Apparently not appreciating this slur on the good health of his neighbour's cow, Edison curled his hands into fists just as Tesla caught sight of his Death Ray in its box.

"Oh my God! Here it is! And just when I need it!"

Picking up the weapon, Tesla whirled on the surprised Edison.

"What the hell is that?"

"Mr. Thomas Alva Edison, may I introduce you to my newest invention! The Tesla Death Ray! My first effort at a directed energy particle-beam weapon!"

As Tesla aimed the weapon at his nemesis, Edison sought cover behind the nearest available object, which I'm sorry to say was me. However, I was frozen into immobility at the sight of Holmes emerging quietly from his bedroom. It was some comfort to me that Holmes appeared to be calm and composed. At least, that was the impression he sought to convey, regardless of what thoughts and emotions were roiling inside him. He glanced at Miss Adler and me in turn, but if he registered any recognition of Miss Adler's striking new outfit, he kept it to himself. Tesla and Edison, however, were oblivious to the appearance of Holmes as they continued their confrontation with one another.

"Tesla! Hold on now! Stop that!"

"Why? Don't you want a practical demonstration? Maybe one hundred thousand volts will jog your memory about the money you owe me!"

"Put it down! Put that down this instant!"

Tesla was clearly enjoying the sight of Edison cringing and cowering before him, as he tracked his every move with the Death Ray.

"Do you know the difference between you and me, Edison?"

"Yes! You're insane and I'm not!"

"No," returned Tesla. "I am a poet and you are not. In fact, would you like to hear the little poem I composed about my Death Ray?

'While listening on my cosmic phone
I caught words from Olympus blown
The latest tells of a cosmic gun
To be pelted is very poor fun!'"

Edison pointed at the advancing Tesla. "You see that? He's crazy! That's why I fired him!"

"You didn't fire me! I quit! It was because of you that I ended up digging ditches in New York for a year!"

Finally spotting Holmes behind Tesla, Edison cried out, "Mr. Holmes! Help me!"

As Tesla turned to look behind him, Holmes took hold of the Death Ray, and using simple leverage combined with his considerable strength, easily removed it from Tesla's hands.

"Calm yourself, Mr. Edison. Mr. Tesla may call this device anything he wishes, but it doesn't actually work."

"What do you mean by that?" asked an incensed Tesla.

"I mean that it is a very elegant design and quite impressive in appearance, but to the best of my knowledge, not functional."

Holmes proceeded to pull the trigger, and the empty clicking sound was audible to everyone in the room. I saw Tesla take in a breath, ready to say something, but then stopping himself. With instantaneous electrocution no longer hovering over his head, Edison was a transformed man, now taking delight in Tesla's discomfiture.

"Oho! What's the problem, Tesla? Cat got your tongue? Now I see! Oh yes! It's another one of your hare-brained schemes, isn't it? Oh, he's got hundreds of them...photographing people's thoughts, building an earthquake machine, and now a Death Ray? Mr. Tesla is a man who is always going to do something amazing, but it's just another mad dream of a madman!"

"'Madman?'" repeated Tesla. "Was it a mad dream when I put an end to your ridiculous plan for using direct current electricity to power entire cities? You would have needed power plants every four blocks and copper cables as thick as my arm!"

"You bastard—" This was clearly still a sore point for Edison.

"Oh, he tried to stop my system from replacing his," continued Tesla, "using my alternating current to electrocute helpless animals, building an electric chair for a prison, and he even tried to get alternating current outlawed!"

"Gentlemen, please!" Holmes held up his hands for silence. "Mr. Edison, you should be aware that just like Mr. Tesla's device, your invention was stolen from your hotel room as well, with a duplicate case left behind. Happily enough, it has also been recovered."

Holmes pointed towards it and Edison immediately rushed for his peculiar device and the photoelectric cell, looking them over anxiously.

"Yes, yes, it's all here! I owe you my eternal thanks, Mr. Holmes!"

I could see that Tesla, with an inventor's curiosity, was regarding Edison's box closely.

"What is it supposed to be?"

"None of your damned business! That's what it's supposed to be!"

"Typical Edison!" replied Tesla with a contemptuous snort. "He assembles an array of nonsense parts, then waits for one of his assistants to create something that actually works so he can take the credit."

"You don't know what you're talking about! The only person who has worked on this is me, and it will remain a secret until I decide to unveil it before the world."

"Oh, I simply love secrets!" chimed in Miss Chartier as she finished her glass of sherry. "They're so exciting! And in my experience, the right kinds of secrets can be most profitable as well, both in the keeping and the revealing. So then, Mr. Edison, let us consider your secret invention. How much will you pay to keep it that way?"

"What? Not a damn thing! You can't bluff me."

"If I might offer a word of advice, Mr. Edison," said Miss Adler, "Miss Chartier doesn't bluff."

"Nonsense! She has no conception of what this is!"

"No?" Miss Chartier ran her finger along the top of Edison's box. "In thinking about it, and adopting the methods of my good friend Sherlock Holmes, I believe that I have deduced my way to the only possible answer. No doubt Mr. Holmes has deduced the very same thing."

The ensuing uncomfortable silence was exceedingly awkward, until I felt compelled to say something. "Well, of course he has! Haven't you, Holmes?"

"No." Holmes gazed around at all of us, like a man about to deliver the eulogy at his own funeral. "Nor did I recover either of your inventions. I am afraid, gentlemen, that I have been riding on my reputation for some time now. I wish it were otherwise, but that is the truth. So, I have been doing some thinking, and I have decided that this case, if it can even be called my case, will be my last. I don't propose to embarrass myself any further and sully what meagre reputation I may have."

"Sweetheart, no..." began Miss Adler. As Holmes waved away her objections, Miss Adler and I shared a glance. This had been our worst fear, that with his deductive abilities at least temporarily dimmed, Holmes would punish both himself and society by retreating from the world.

"Time moves on," continued Holmes. "Better to retire gracefully now than to be revealed as a charlatan and a fool. I couldn't bear that. I remain a great lover of facts, and the fact is that I've had my day, but that day is gone."

The lump in my throat felt the size of an apple, even as I became aware of someone clapping. It was Marie Chartier.

"I do not know what you are playing at Mr. Holmes, but you would have made a rare actor. You seriously expect me to believe a word you just said?"

"Believe what you like," answered Holmes. "In the meantime, since you have borrowed my methods and put them to better use than I can, I would be most grateful if you would explain the intricacies of Mr. Edison's machine. What is it?"

"The only thing it can be." Knowing that she had the room in the palm of her hand, Miss Chartier paused to refill her sherry glass, took a sip, then regarded us with an easy smile.

"There is a logical chain that leads to only one conclusion. What do we know of Thomas Edison? Where did he get his start in inventing? With the telegraph machine. No, he did not invent it, but he worked on it relentlessly, making it better and more efficient. He was obsessed with communication using Morse Code. And when Alexander Graham Bell invented the telephone, who made it functional over large distances with his carbon transmitter? None other than Mr. Edison. Again, obsessed with a communication device."

She regarded Edison's mystery invention with what appeared to be genuine affection.

"And what do we have here? A beam of infrared light, a photoelectric cell, and a receiver. Presumably, when the beam is broken, this red bulb lights up. Ah, but it cannot be broken by just any kind of interference. No, Mr. Edison has gone to great pains to ensure that the light will only be activated should the beam be broken by something of a particular density or electrical charge. Should that be achieved, and the light goes on, then perhaps messages can be sent and received using Morse Code."

Whatever contempt Edison may have held for Miss Chartier a minute ago, it was rapidly dissipating as she spoke.

"Miss Chartier, you really don't have to go on."

"Oh, I think I do."

"I will pay you handsomely if you do not."

Miss Chartier nodded. "And there you have it. The last and most important clue to revealing the purpose of this device. Thomas Edison is famous for trumpeting his achievements from every rooftop. He wants his name on everything and longs for fame and recognition. Except now. This device is the only exception to that rule. It is Edison's secret invention. And why? Why should he fear the public learning what he has devoted so much time and effort to?"

"Miss Chartier, please..." Edison was now clearly in some degree of distress.

"Because he would be ruined. He would become the laughingstock of the scientific community unless he could prove that it works, which he has yet to do."

If nothing else, Miss Chartier's recitation had piqued my curiosity to a fever pitch. "For God's sake, what is it?"

"It's clearly a communication device," said Miss Adler.

"Yes," confirmed Miss Chartier.

"Well, how does it work?" I asked. "Whom does it communicate with?"

Draining her sherry glass, Miss Chartier proceeded to throw it into the fireplace, where it shattered into glistening shards before she turned back to us, her eyes shining.

"The dead."

Chapter Six

The Second Secret Revealed

I wasn't sure that I had heard Miss Chartier correctly, and so I instinctively turned to Holmes for confirmation as I always did, but he was clearly as lost as I was.

Miss Chartier continued, "It is a spirit phone. A Ghost Machine, if you will. A device to reach into the realm beyond..."

We all turned to Edison. Like a cornered rat, he peered at us with angry and suspicious eyes.

"Yes," he began quietly. "That is exactly what it is. And this invention is mine and mine alone. It's not an improvement or reworking of someone else's idea. It's mine from start to finish. But I can't afford to let it be publicised before I can prove that it works. I would be ruined. Dismissed as a complete crackpot. So go ahead, Tesla. Make your jokes. I'm sure you're aching to have a laugh at my expense."

Picking up Edison's photoelectric cell to examine it, Tesla shook his head.

"By no means. On the contrary, I am most intrigued. After all, everything we do with electricity is predicated upon things that we cannot see...electrons moving this way and that, and the use of magnetic fields. Or consider the invisible viruses that constantly surround us. Day by day, it becomes clearer that we live in the midst of worlds we cannot perceive. I commend you for your scientific curiosity."

"Seriously?" Edison appeared to be stunned by Tesla's words.

"Allow me to tell you something," Tesla went on. "The most remarkable person I have ever known is my own mother. She was truly a great woman, of rare skill, courage, and fortitude.

She was also an inventor of the first order. Most of the clothes and furnishings of our home were the product of her own hand. When she was past sixty, her fingers were still nimble enough to tie three knots in an eyelash, and I have never had the sense of connection that I had with my mother with any other human being. On the day that she died, five thousand miles away in Serbia, she came to me in a dream to tell me that she loved me. I knew she had passed on before any official word came. How? I have no idea. But perhaps Mr. Edison's machine can provide the answer."

Snatching the photoelectric cell from Tesla's hand, Miss Adler walked to the centre of the room. "Hold on. Just hold on one minute. Do I have this right? I'm listening to Thomas Edison claiming that he can talk to ghosts on the telephone?"

"I'm not!" answered Edison, incensed by Miss Adler's goading comment. "Make no mistake! I have no time for spiritualism or the supernatural. It's all hogwash! I believe in science and measurable, repeatable results. I am not unlike Mr. Holmes in that I believe that the secrets of nature can be revealed through experimentation and observation."

"How can a Ghost Machine possibly be scientific?" I exclaimed. "That's absurd!"

"I beg to differ," Edison paused for a moment to compose his thoughts. "I will attempt to explain it to you, but if a single word of this gets outside these rooms, I swear to God I will sue each and every one of you into oblivion. Now then, I have been thinking for some time of a machine or apparatus that could be operated by personalities which have passed on to another existence or sphere. My theory is that the electrons that create our consciousness and make up our memories don't perish with death, but still exist and can be detected and measured. Maybe only for a short time, but if these bits of matter, what I call 'life units,' are electron-based, then they would give off a negative charge. So, what if a cohesive bundle of negatively charged particles crossed through a tightly focused field of photons—a beam of light. If they did, they should generate an interference with the photon stream and register a form of electric charge on a receiving cell or meter. Perhaps there could even be communication. One registration on the meter means yes. Two means no. As Miss Chartier suggested, Morse Code could even be used."

"I see what you are saying!" said Tesla. "In fact, I just read a paper by a young German physicist named Einstein on what he calls his Theory of Special Relativity. He claims that matter cannot be created or destroyed. It only changes form. Mass becomes energy and nothing really fades out of existence. So, what you are saying is that upon death human consciousness merely changes form, and you're redefining the concept of a ghost from something spiritual into something electrical; that is, the cohesive remains of a consciousness."

"Yes, exactly!" Edison nodded his agreement. "Make no mistake Tesla, you're an arrogant and irritating son-of-a-bitch, but I'm glad you're here because you understand the theories that I'm working with. Our cells have memory, as in when you cut yourself and the body heals. And I believe that memory resides in our electrons as life units, independent of the body, so that our personalities persist in an electronic state after death."

"And they would naturally exit the body after death and pass into another habitat," Tesla mused, "like a virus spreading to a new host."

"Good Lord!" I exclaimed, not certain I understood everything that was being said, but understanding enough to know that what Edison was proposing would change the world as we knew it. "Well, that would explain the idea of reincarnation, if these life units somehow reformed themselves into memories in new bodies."

"Perhaps," hedged Edison. "We shall see. This machine is designed to open a valve to another realm. Just as a microscope allows biologists to observe organisms not visible to the naked eye, we will be able to detect cohesions of electrons, a migration of the soul, not on a spiritual level, but on a bioelectrical level."

After sitting in silence listening to Edison's quite incredible speculations, Holmes finally spoke.

"That's all very well in theory, Mr. Edison, but you say you haven't conducted a successful demonstration yet?"

"No. But in my profession, I consider every failure to be a success, because it eliminates another possibility. This is the most sensitive apparatus I have ever undertaken to build, but there is one factor outside of my control."

"Which is?"

"Somehow summoning a recently departed spirit to cross the beam of infrared light."

"Well, that solves both mysteries regarding the purpose of these inventions," said Miss Adler. "Now, only one mystery remains. What is your interest in this, Miss Chartier? And please don't pretend that you have any intention of helping the British government."

"Is it not obvious?" Miss Chartier looked around the room, but what was obvious to her had apparently eluded everyone else. "These inventions are devoted to life and death. To possess both, and the profits they would generate, would be the greatest monopoly of all. I believe it was after our second bottle of champagne at The Savoy that Mr. Tesla graciously shared with me the full potential of his Death Ray..."

"Did I? I have no recollection of that."

"You were drunk, my dear Nikola, as I fully intended you should be. Fortunately, like you, I have a curiously retentive memory, and you were most eloquent and passionate when describing your device, invoking images of Zeus hurling down thunderbolts from Mt. Olympus."

Miss Chartier picked up the weapon and cradled it in her arms like a newborn child. "This is but a prototype, an infant Death Ray if you will. The fully developed weapon will be thousands of times more powerful. Against it no nation or army could survive. It is an engine of annihilation. Entire cities would be reduced to beds of whitened ashes and every living thing would be exterminated. Lightning would pour from the sky, and the charred and fire-shriveled bodies of soldiers would fall helpless before its irresistible force. London, Paris, and New York could all be reduced to blackened, smoking, lifeless ruins within a matter of hours."

"But no!" Tesla took his weapon away from Miss Chartier in a state of considerable agitation. "You mustn't say that! Miss Chartier, please, you are labouring under a misapprehension. My Death Ray, once perfected, will never be used! Indeed, it might more accurately be called a Peace Ray. Imagine every country around the world with an array of these at their border, an invisible Great Wall of China, only a million times more impenetrable against any attack or invasion."

I was struggling to follow this, and said as much. "You're saying, Mr. Tesla, that this is a weapon of peace?"

"Yes!" Tesla nodded emphatically. "My father was a minister and a devoted pacifist, as am I. What he believed, and what I believe, is that we need closer contact and better understanding between individuals and communities all over the earth, and the elimination of that fanatic devotion to exalted ideals of nationalism, which is always prone to plunge the world into primeval barbarism and strife. The ultimate purpose of my device, therefore, is to end all human conflict, and I wish nothing more than to be remembered as the inventor who abolished war."

The irony of what Tesla was saying, a weapon whose only purpose is to abolish war, was not lost on me. Nor apparently on Miss Chartier, who burst into laughter.

"Oh, Nikola. I do love your optimism, however naive and childish it might be. Name me one weapon that mankind has invented and then never used? We have the minds of gods, but the emotions of reptiles. We love to kill...to destroy. It runs in our blood like a fever. Have you looked around Europe recently? Every country is an armed camp, everyone ready to launch into all-out war at a moment's notice for the sake of honour or patriotism or whatever excuse needs to be found. Perhaps not this year or next. But it is coming—a great, global war like the world has never seen, with ferocious new weapons never before used.

"The young men on both sides will be drawn from the fields and the factories, excited at the prospect of being a soldier. They will be told what they are always told, that their cause is just, that God is on their side, and that it will be a short and glorious war. And they will gladly give up their lives for coloured pieces of ribbon and shiny bits of metal because they all want to be heroes. And they will be. The German heroes will kill the French heroes. The British heroes will kill the Bulgarian heroes. The Austrian heroes will kill the American heroes. And the rotting of heroic corpses will create a heroic stench that will drift up to the heavens to delight their bloodthirsty gods. Yes, the mothers and wives and daughters will weep, as they always do. But no matter. A few years will pass, a new crop of heroes will be born, and the slaughter will go on as it always has. And somewhere, far from the front lines, men in suits will count their profits and make a toast to the next great war. Better yet, a war that begins and never ends."

"That's utterly obscene!" I cried out. "What you're saying is an insult to our gallant young men in uniform!"

"All the young men are gallant, no matter what uniform they wear," returned Miss Chartier. "And in the end, their corpses are indistinguishable from one another. You were in the Second Anglo-Afghan War, Doctor. Was it glorious? Come now. Tell us the truth about war. About the shining young faces of the men going to the front. Was it glorious, Dr. Watson, when the shattered bodies of those same young men were brought back to you on stretchers? In pieces? In tears? Their minds as broken as their bodies?"

"No," I finally managed. "It's more horrible than you can possibly imagine. Men weeping and screaming on the battlefield, trying to scoop their own intestines back into their bodies, calling out for their mothers or their wives, taking hours or even days to die. The scenes of suffering and carnage were monstrous."

"Because war is monstrous," agreed Miss Chartier. "But if it is inevitable, if men, in their infinite wisdom, should see fit to fabricate one war after another, why should I not profit from it? Which brings us to the beautiful synchronicity of Tesla's Death Ray and Edison's Ghost Machine. Soon enough, there will be too many corpses to count and families desperate to contact a dead son, a dead brother, a dead father. Just imagine the immense size of the market of the bereaved. The Death Ray will take the young men from their families and the Ghost Machine will bring them back. Now that, my friends, is a business model for the ages."

The staggering cynicism of Miss Chartier's views on war and humanity were bad enough, but compounded by the fact that all of us simply fell silent, unable to offer up any kind of counterargument. If she intended to prey upon the fears and foolishness of mankind and then profit from perpetual warfare and countless deaths, she would soon be a very wealthy woman indeed. Still, there was one potential fly in her ointment, and it was Holmes who pointed it out.

"Well, I suppose all we can say is, thank God Tesla's weapon doesn't work."

"But it does!" objected Tesla. "I assure you that it is a simple matter of projecting concentrated non-dispersive energy through natural media!"

"What the hell is that supposed to mean?" scoffed Edison. "Your little toy doesn't work, Tesla, and there's no point in pretending otherwise."

Tesla looked down at the Death Ray in his hands. "Oh, blind, faint-hearted, doubting world. It moves slowly, and new truths are difficult to see. Yes, it is true, my enemies have succeeded in painting me as an amusing wizard of sorts, whose ambition constantly exceeds his reach. I will concede to you, Edison, that the present is yours..."

"Thank you!" returned Edison.

"But the future is mine!" With that, Tesla slid open a secret compartment in the Death Ray by some combination of pressure from his fingers and thumb. Removing a disc of metal, he proceeded to toss it to Edison.

"What's this?" asked the baffled Edison.

"A magnetron," answered Tesla. "But one of insufficient strength to operate the weapon. I put it there in case it should fall into the wrong hands. Call it a little bit of misdirection. The weapon requires a magnetron of considerably more power to work; specifically, a magnetron composed of tungsten. A magnetron like this..."

Reaching into his jacket, Tesla pulled out another disc of metal, and with a rapid motion inserted it into the weapon and closed the secret compartment. Almost instantly, we heard the Death Ray start up with an electric whine. Tesla smiled and closed his eyes.

"Do you hear that sound, my friends? That is the sound of peace for mankind."

Marie Chartier darted forward and pulled the weapon from Tesla's hands.

"Or not. I do apologise, my dear Nikola, but the simple fact is that peace is not very profitable. War, on the other hand, is where fortunes are made."

"What are you doing?" Tesla was mystified by Miss Chartier's actions.

"What I have been commissioned to do by the British government. I need to verify that your Death Ray actually works."

"Miss Chartier, please! It is a very sensitive device! Put it down!"

"And the Kaiser was most particular on that point as well—is Tesla's Death Ray fully functional?"

"Wait a moment!" I interjected. "You mean to say that you've been in contact with the German government?"

"I mean to say that I am open to offers from the highest bidder," returned Miss Chartier coolly. "You may accuse me of duplicity if you wish, but there is no question in my mind that Mycroft Holmes knows precisely where my allegiance lies, which has nothing to do with this or that country, and everything to do with my bank account. Besides, he deals with diplomats regularly, so quite naturally he assumes everyone will lie to him. In other words, he expects me to double-cross him, but imagines himself clever enough to stop me."

"But you can't possibly mean to use Tesla's device!" said Edison.

"Oh no? Look at you, Mr. Edison, afraid of a little experimentation! Where was that fear when you were electrocuting dogs and prisoners to try to discredit Tesla's alternating current technology?"

"That..." Edison was caught completely off guard by Miss Chartier's accusation. "That wasn't me! That was a man named Harry Brown! It was Harry Brown who did that! And he was behind the electric chair too!"

Miss Chartier shook her head. "Could you possibly be any more pathetic? Wasting your breath on ridiculous lies. Who do you think you are talking to? I am the daughter of Professor Moriarty. I live by one rule—do what you can get away with. And that is the rule you live by as well, Mr. Edison. That is the rule by which you made your name. Admit it."

"No! That's not true! I'm a respectable businessman and inventor!"

Miss Chartier turned the Death Ray towards Edison and he backed away from her, his face going white.

"You are making this very easy for me," she declared.

"Making what easy?"

"To verify that Tesla's Death Ray works I need to choose its first victim. And if you persist in your foolish and insulting denials it will be you. You were behind the electrocution campaign in New York, doing what you always do. Presenting the innocent face of Thomas Edison the great inventor to the world, but lying, cheating, and scheming behind the scenes."

I could see Edison glancing frantically to his left and right, looking for some way out, but Miss Chartier tracked his every move with the Death Ray. He was well and truly trapped and would meet the same fate as those helpless electrocuted animals unless he told Miss Chartier what she wanted to hear.

"I was proving a point!" Edison finally exclaimed. "Tesla's system was a public menace and the public deserved to know! There's no crime in that!"

"Oh, actually there is," said Miss Chartier. "Many, many crimes, in fact. But I'm so glad you recognise how similar we are, Mr. Edison. However, that still leaves me with the problem of choosing the Death Ray's first victim. Who shall it be?"

In turn, Miss Chartier aimed the weapon at Tesla, Edison, Holmes, and then me.

"Its own creator?...His hated rival?...Perhaps the detective who can no longer detect?...Or the writer with no more stories to write? No. None of those. I need to commit the perfect murder..." she aimed the Death Ray at Miss Adler, "...and there is only one person in this room who is already officially dead. That would be you, Miss Adler, thanks to Dr. Watson killing you off in 'A Scandal in Bohemia.' And I can't very well be accused of murdering a dead woman now, can I?"

"Miss Chartier," Holmes stepped towards her and she leveled the gun at him, "you wouldn't…"

"Wouldn't I? Where was that thought when you threw my father off the Reichenbach waterfall? Where was your empathy then, Mr. Holmes? Or do you only care when it is someone you love who is about to die? Either all life is precious, or none of it is. So which is it?"

If Holmes had a good answer to that question, we never got to hear it, for at that moment Miss Adler lunged at Miss Chartier in an effort to wrest the Death Ray from her hands. Like a ballerina, Miss Chartier simply spun in a circle and then pointed the weapon at Miss Adler, who was now completely at her mercy. For a moment that seemed to last a lifetime, we all simply stared, frozen in place, and then with a crackle of energy a white bolt of electric fire emerged from the barrel of the gun and Miss Adler was thrown back into the arms of Holmes as if she had been kicked by a horse. As she collapsed against Holmes like a rag doll, Edison made a dash for the door, followed closely by Tesla. Dropping the Death Ray, Miss Chartier was only steps behind them as Holmes lowered the limp Miss Adler to the floor.

"Watson! Do something!" cried Holmes.

Running into my bedroom, I was back in a moment with my medical bag and at Miss Adler's side. As I waved a small ammonia bottle beneath her nose, Holmes arose and backed away. Scrambling in my bag for a heart stimulant, I tipped the bottle between Miss Adler's lips, only to watch the dark liquid run from her mouth and onto the floor.

"Watson!" I could hear the panic and fear in Holmes' voice. "For God's sake!"

Lifting up one of her eyelids with no response, I felt for a pulse on her wrist, but after a moment or two looked up at Holmes and said the only thing I could say.

"She's gone, Holmes..."

Holmes and I looked at one another in silence, each of us lost in our own thoughts, our world irrevocably changed within the span of a single heartbeat.

Chapter Seven
The Mysterious Mystery

The following three days were a blur of everything and nothing. As Miss Adler lay motionless on the floor after being struck by Tesla's Death Ray, Holmes had backed away in horror and disbelief. Just before he collapsed on the divan, he gazed about the room in a kind of panic, as if he were trying to memorise the scene even as he could feel himself going into shock.

"Nothing must be moved, Watson!" he cried. "Promise me that! Nothing must be touched!"

With that, a wave of unconsciousness mercifully swept over him. Making sure he was as comfortable as possible, I slipped a pillow beneath Holmes' head and covered him with a blanket. I then contacted Mycroft to tell him everything that had happened, and I also explained to him his brother's insistence that the room be left just as it was. Mycroft agreed that would be best, and to my relief indicated that he would communicate the situation to Tesla and Edison.

For whatever reason, Tesla's Death Ray had ceased making its electric pulsing sound when Miss Chartier dropped it to the floor, and it was my fervent wish that the infernal device was broken beyond repair. Still, I made sure to keep well clear of it, as well as Edison's Ghost Machine, as I crept like a mouse back and forth through the room to check on Holmes, who simply lay on the divan, drifting in and out of sleep. Every so often I endeavoured to bring him something to drink or eat, but all he could manage was a little water now and then, before disappearing back into whatever nightmares he was experiencing, as I would occasionally hear him call out Miss

Adler's name, or even engage her in some kind of incomprehensible conversation. On this particular morning, I ascended our stairs as quietly as I could, bearing a tray with a pot of tea and some biscuits. I didn't want to disturb Holmes unduly, but I was going to insist that he at least try a biscuit or two to help keep his strength up.

Entering our room, I put the tray down, took out my pocket watch, then grasped Holmes' wrist to measure his pulse. In the previous days I had often found it shallow and quick, but now I was somewhat reassured to find it steady and quite normal. As I counted the beats against the seconds on my watch, Holmes suddenly spoke.

"I'm awake, Watson."

"Finally. Thank God."

Opening his eyes, Holmes took in the room and the light streaming through our window. "What time is it?"

"Nine in the morning. Saturday." Holmes looked at me questioningly. "You've had a bad fever, brought on by shock, no doubt. You've been slipping in and out of consciousness for three days now. Here...try to sit up and get some tea into you."

As Holmes struggled into a sitting position, I poured him a cup of tea, wondering just how much he recalled of the terrible events that had led to his collapse.

"Do you remember...?"

"Irene is dead. Yes, I remember." Holmes gazed around the room, seeing both Tesla's Death Ray and Edison's Ghost Machine. "Our inventors have not returned for their devices?"

"No," I answered. "You told me that nothing should be touched."

"So I did." I could see Holmes trying to cast his mind back to the terrible night in question.

"And Irene…has she…?"

Holmes looked up at me with a haunted expression, and I knew what question he couldn't bear to ask.

"Yes. East Highgate Cemetery."

"Ah, East Highgate. Is she near George Eliot, do you know?"

"I don't believe so. It's a quiet little corner near the Chester Road gate. I'm afraid that at the insistence of your brother, it's an unmarked grave."

"Of course it is. And may I assume that Mycroft swept all other troublesome details under the rug?"

"Yes."

"Is there anything else I should know?"

"No," I answered. "I've simply been keeping an eye on you, listening to you call out Miss Adler's name in your delirium."

"And she has been here."

Handing Holmes his tea, I resisted the urge to ask him if I might take his temperature, although it was clear to me that he was still suffering from some degree of brain fever.

Holmes sipped his tea. "She comes to me as a shadow, speaks to me quietly, lays her hand on my head, and then she is gone."

Holmes picked up a biscuit and glanced at me. "Don't worry, old friend. I know it's only a dream…my mind creating what I want to be real. I imagine I will have those dreams for some time until they fade away…as everything fades away." Holmes took a bite of biscuit and continued, "Mind you, I'm not saying there is nothing of substance in Edison's claims. Perhaps his notion of 'life units' has some merit, but that would have to be established scientifically."

Relieved to hear Holmes speaking more rationally, I freshened his tea.

"Yes. You're quite right, of course. Can I get you anything besides tea and biscuits? Something more substantial? A drink? Maybe you'd like to go for a walk? How about a newspaper? Which would you prefer, 'The Times' or 'The Daily Telegraph'? Both perhaps?"

Holmes leaned back on the divan and closed his eyes. I could see rapid side-to-side movement beneath his eyelids, and when his eyes snapped open again there was a hard sheen to them, and an expression that I hadn't seen in quite some time.

"Out with it, old boy."

"Out with what?"

"I have been lying here three days. That has given you ample time to consider what you will say now that I'm awake. No doubt your lines are well-rehearsed by this point, so say what you want to say."

Holmes was absolutely correct, of course. The loss of Miss Adler had left Holmes literally prostrate with grief, and in tending to him I had more than sufficient time to muse over what things would be like when he finally recovered his senses. I had my hopes, of course, but more than that, I had any number of fears, but I was disinclined to inflict those upon Holmes at this very moment.

"It can wait," I said.

"No, it can't," answered Holmes. "Life, as was so recently demonstrated, is a temporary condition. None of us has as much time as we imagine. Out with it."

Mustering up my nerve as best I could, I cleared my throat. "Well, the fact of the matter is, I do want to talk to you about something. And this may sound tremendously unfeeling of me, but...perhaps tomorrow would be a better day."

"Everything you are about to say has already crossed my mind. Get yourself a brandy to steady your nerves and then get on with it."

The fact is, I did need a brandy, and although I could have objected that I didn't and that it wasn't even noon yet, instead I went to the sideboard and poured myself a healthy snifter. Taking a large swallow, I let the warmth of the liquid permeate my insides, then turned back to Holmes for what I was certain would be a highly unpleasant, but necessary conversation.

"Very well. Holmes, let me be frank. I was here with you before Miss Adler entered our lives. What I saw was often not very pretty. And with her gone...in your current state of mind, I can't help but be concerned that you're going to reach for comfort where it cannot be found."

"In the needle and syringe, you mean. Is this really the best time for a lecture, Doctor?"

"Let me just read you something from one of my old notebooks." With Holmes incapacitated for three days, I had dug it out to have at hand when this particular conversation took place. I picked it up and began reading.

"'Dreadful day. The worst yet. Holmes is three weeks without a case and his mental and physical conditions are deteriorating rapidly. The vein in his right arm is quite collapsed and he hasn't eaten in four days. Having consulted with Dr. Phelps, we are going to have Holmes forcibly removed to Bartholomew's Hospital in an effort to save his life.'"

"That's not true!" Holmes objected. "That never happened! I have never been admitted to Bartholomew's Hospital."

"No. Because that evening the King of Bohemia appeared in these rooms and the very next day you made the acquaintance of Irene Adler."

"Ah. Yes, I do recall I was at a bit of a low ebb at the time."

"To put it mildly," I agreed. "And since that day, would you care to sum up for me your drug use? How many injections? How many pills?"

"None," replied Holmes. "So please do me the kindness of allowing me to board the train bound for the destination to which your logic is inexorably headed. With Irene gone, I need a woman. I need a woman or I will become a raving drug addict."

It was both comforting and more than a little alarming that Holmes was able to predict what I was going to say so accurately.

"I'm not saying this week or next month or next year, even! I'm saying—"

"No."

"Damn it, Holmes! You're the logical one! I mean no disrespect to Miss Adler's memory, but you have to look at this logically!"

"No. And again no. And finally, no. Now if you don't mind, I think I'll join you in a brandy."

I had told myself that I wasn't going to be intimidated by Holmes' words or manner, so as he made his way to the sideboard I tossed my old notebook aside and followed after him.

"I am not going to stand by and watch you killing yourself again! I'm not. It's one thing to mourn the dead. It is quite another to mourn someone who is still living. And that is what it means to live with a drug addict. To watch a man you respect and admire above all others destroying himself, disappearing before your very eyes...I won't have it. You put another needle in your arm and I swear to God I will kill you myself!" Having poured his drink, Holmes turned to me and our eyes locked. "I mean what I say, Holmes."

"I know." Sipping his brandy, Holmes moved to his armchair and sat down. There was clearly something that he wanted to say, but he wasn't quite sure how to say it. All I could do was sit on the divan and wait, so that is precisely what I did. Taking another sip, Holmes held his glass up to the light, gazing into it as if it were a crystal ball.

"Watson, I want to tell you something...something that I don't want to ever appear in one of your tales for 'The Strand Magazine.' I know you will find this difficult to believe, but when I was a child I was considered somewhat peculiar. By my classmates, by my teachers, by my own parents even. I was different, and God knows how much the world despises difference. So I kept to myself, reading, studying, engaging in little experiments of all kinds. But then I got a little older and to my own astonishment found that there was a girl who lived nearby that I rather fancied.

"Auburn hair, dark brown eyes, and the tiniest little scar above her left cheekbone, which I found absolutely enchanting. And by some miracle of willpower I worked up the courage to ask her to accompany me to a school dance. And she laughed. And then she told her friends and they laughed. Word spread, as it does in a small village, and apparently the very idea of me taking a girl to a dance was the most ridiculous thing in the world."

"Oh, Holmes. I'm so sorry..."

"No, it was a blessing. Because it allowed me to close that side of myself up. Completely and utterly. Put a chain around your heart and you will find, ironically enough, that you are free. Free to not care. To not want. Not desire. And it enabled me, much like our friend Tesla, to focus obsessively on my rather singular profession...to become the world's first consulting detective...a calculating machine. And that was an absolute joy...to pour myself, every ounce of my being into crime, into mysteries that no one else could fathom or untangle...until a day or two passed with no case or scheming villain and I could feel myself starting to unravel. I needed work, and if there was no work, then..."

"Drugs."

"Yes. Until the day Miss Adler entered our lives. As you just noted I was not in a particularly good state at the time. I was weak, damaged...vulnerable. The self-control that had kept that chain so tightly wrapped around my heart had slipped. I was like a helpless, newborn baby chick, and the vision of Miss Adler imprinted itself on my mind and soul. I needed, wanted, and loved her more than I imagined I could ever love anything or anyone. But that moment, that once in a lifetime moment, is gone, never to return...which is why my answer to you is no."

I was more than touched by this revelation from Holmes, whose youth and private life had always been a closed book, even to me, his chronicler and closest friend. Still, seeing him this candid and open, I knew I would never have a better chance to press my point with the hope of having some influence on him.

"I'm not suggesting that any woman could possibly replace Miss Adler, but a few female friends and an occasional evening out would do you a world of good. There are quite literally thousands of women in London who would be beyond delighted to make your acquaintance."

"And no matter how bright or kind or beautiful any of those women might be, they would all suffer from one fatal flaw. Not one of them would be Irene."

"But Holmes, you must—"

"No, no, no," Holmes said in a calm, quiet voice. "You needn't worry. I won't be reaching for the needle. All I care about now is what would make Irene happy...what would make her proud of me. You see, I have her constantly in my mind. She is a part of me, now and forever. And if you should happen to see me talking to myself about a case, please know that I am actually talking to her."

"A case?" The last word I had expected to hear from Holmes at this moment certainly caught my attention. "Then you're not retiring?"

"Not a bit of it," Holmes finished his brandy. "From this moment on I shall devote myself to being a productive and responsible citizen. The injured and the preyed upon may depend on me as an ally, and I hereby pledge my remaining years to being a tireless advocate for truth and justice. Irene's memory deserves no less."

I could hardly believe my ears. Whatever fears I may have had regarding this particular conversation, they had now been put to rest.

"I'm very relieved to hear that, Holmes. You're doing the right thing. It really is the only path that will make you happy."

"Happy? Oh, Watson. That ship has sailed, my friend."

"Don't say that."

"But I do. Allow me to quote the American writer Ralph Waldo Emerson. 'The purpose of life it not to be happy. It is to be useful, to be honourable, to be compassionate, to have it make some difference that you have lived and lived well.'"

"Hear, hear!" I agreed, finishing my brandy and making my way to the mantel. I held up the pile of letters that Holmes had received from people all over the globe seeking his help. "Which means we need a case!"

Getting to his feet, Holmes took the letters from my hand. "These can wait. We have a much more important case to consider; indeed, it is the most important case of my career."

"What case is that?"

Picking up his jackknife, Holmes pinned the letters to the mantel with a savage thrust and turned to me. "We need to solve the murder of Irene Adler!"

"The...?" I felt a cold chill crawling up my spine. Everything had been going so well and Holmes had seemed like his old self, but now I was wondering just how much the fever had affected his brain. "I'm not sure I know what you mean."

"No?" Holmes picked up a biscuit and began eating it as I scrambled to order my thoughts as best I could.

"We were both here!" I began. "It was in this room! Marie Chartier shot Miss Adler with Tesla's Death Ray. We watched it happen!"

"Did we?"

"Holmes, you're worrying me."

Holmes began to pace back and forth, finishing one biscuit and then immediately taking another one.

"Things are not that simple! You involve the British and German governments, my brother Mycroft, and Marie Chartier and the complexity of events expand a thousand-fold. There is genius here, Watson, I am sure of it! I believe that we saw what we were intended to see, and there is often a vast gulf between what we think happened and what actually happened. What we witnessed was nothing less than the very end of an intricately planned conspiracy. What we need to do now is reason backwards to get to the conspirators themselves!"

Hearing Holmes talk in this fashion was alarming in the extreme. What he needed was a good old-fashioned kidnapping or bank robbery to focus his attention on. All this talk about a conspiracy was the last thing I wanted to hear.

"Holmes," I began, "you clearly need to get a bit more rest. Let me—"

"No, Watson! I am as awake as I have ever been! Every ounce of my deductive faculties is on fire! So let the investigation begin!"

"Begin where?"

"Excellent question! Excellent question from my comrade in arms. Excellent question indeed! So then, let me ask you this...how would you characterise the measurement of one inch?"

"I'm sorry?"

"One inch! How would you characterise it? Would you say that it is a large measurement or a small measurement? My God, these biscuits are marvellous!"

For Holmes, the whiff of a conspiracy theory was like a bull being presented with the red cape of a matador. I concluded that my best option at this point would be to play along and let Holmes charge and charge again until he had exhausted himself and could get a bit more sleep.

"Well," I began, "that would depend on..."

"Depend on what? What would it depend on? Out with it!"

"The context."

"Excellent! We're already closer, aren't we? Logic, you see? Inexorable logic, Watson. That is the key. Now. This context of yours. Do go on! You fascinate me."

"What I mean is, obviously if you're talking about, say, a carriage ride through Hyde Park, one inch is a completely inconsequential distance..."

"It is, isn't it? Absolutely inconsequential! I couldn't agree more! We're clearly thinking along the same lines, old friend! And now...?"

"Now...?" I could feel the thread of this rather bizarre conversation slipping from my grasp.

"The other end! The other end, Watson! We look at things from both ends! Back to front! Front to back! The answer is in the details!"

"You've lost me," I admitted.

"When is an inch consequential? When does it matter?"

"Well, if it's a bullet wound, for example. Or a piece of shrapnel. One inch either way can be the difference between life and death."

"Exactly!" Holmes shoved the last remaining biscuit into his mouth. "The difference between life and death! That is the meaning of a single inch!"

Having worked up a thirst from his biscuit consumption, Holmes proceeded to pour himself another cup of tea.

"Ah, I see," I offered. "Yes, I see what you mean. But I'm not quite sure how this gets us any closer to solving Miss Adler's murder."

"Of course not. No. I'm jumping ahead, which is a capital mistake. We must build our case, Watson. Build our case from the ground up. You're absolutely right. We must take the most logical step first. So, step one...how will we discover who murdered Irene?"

Having momentarily felt myself to be back on solid ground, I just as quickly found it slipping away from under my feet.

"I'm afraid I don't know."

"Isn't it obvious? Think of the most obvious thing in the world that we can do! It's ludicrously simple! I'll give you ten seconds to think it over!"

More than a little rattled by Holmes' manic state, he may as well have given me ten hours or ten months and I still wouldn't have been able to come up with anything resembling a coherent answer. As the seconds counted down, Holmes approached me, until his face was mere inches from mine.

"Time's up, old fellow! But never fear, Sherlock Holmes is here! So then, how will we expose Irene's murderer?"

"I have no idea," I answered.

"We'll ask her!"

Chapter Eight
A Most Peculiar Investigation

From the moment Holmes had awoken from his shock-induced stupor, I had been conscious of walking a conversational tightrope. There were moments when everything seemed to be quite steady and normal, then would come an unsettling tremor or two. But Holmes' suggestion that we interview Miss Adler regarding her own murder completely unbalanced me.

"Ask Miss Adler?" I repeated.

"Yes! Look what we have here! Edison's Ghost Machine! His theories are sound! Miss Adler is only recently deceased and she died in this very room! At this moment her life units surround us in bioelectrical form, only we cannot see or detect them! Think of it! She wants to communicate with us, Watson, and we will give her that chance!"

My heart sank. It had always been Holmes' energy and single-minded focus that had served him so well in our cases, and I knew there was little chance of dissuading him from the course he had just suggested. It was like being in a room with a runaway locomotive, and as it bore down on me all I could do was hold up my hands.

"Holmes, please. You're not—"

"So this is what we are going to do," Holmes spoke right over me. "We need to gather everyone who was here on that night. I want you to bring Tesla, Edison, and Miss Chartier here."

"I'm not sure I can make that happen."

"We will make it happen!"

"But for what purpose?"

"Watson, we are going to hold a séance! Right here. On the very spot Irene Adler died. Tomorrow night at precisely eight o'clock. We will set up Edison's machine and summon Irene's spirit to join us. And we must do it quickly, because we don't know how long her life units will remain in this proximity. It would be an affront to science itself if we didn't take advantage of this opportunity, because we have the perfect conditions to test Edison's theory. Now, what do I need to do next?"

"I'm sure I don't know."

"I need to go out. Out into the bustling maelstrom of human joy and misery that is London. The whole of human knowledge is out there, if only one knows where to look! And I, my dutiful chronicler, I am very good at looking! Now, I shall be in and out because there is much to learn and do. You shall arrange the séance for tomorrow night and I am going to insist that you follow my directions precisely. Will you do that?"

"What directions?"

"Do you happen to recall our rule for taking cabs in times of danger or peril?"

"Yes, of course," I replied. "Never take the first or second cab. It may be a trap."

"Exactly! Well, I think it is fair to say that these circumstances and the conspiracy behind them necessitate more extreme measures. Given that, I am going to request that you forgo all manner of public conveyance. Make your way around London on foot and be absolute certain that you are not being followed. Gather up our principals however you may, but it is essential that Tesla, Edison, and Miss Chartier attend our séance so that the truth may be revealed!"

Holmes headed towards our door, only pausing to fling on his hat and coat, and then he was gone. Immediately rushing to the window, I had four aims in mind. First and foremost, I needed to keep my wits about me. Following that, I needed to give Holmes a decent head start, see in which direction he was headed, and then dog his footsteps for the remainder of the day. In his current state of mind there was no way of predicting what he might say or do, so it was imperative that I not only protect Holmes, but protect other people from Holmes. As for the assignment Holmes had given me regarding gathering up attendees for his proposed séance, I would simply have to address that as best I could as the day unfolded.

Emerging out onto Baker Street, I could see that Holmes was already a good fifty yards down the road. I began walking after him, and it was everything I could do to keep up with Holmes' long stride and purposeful pace. Making a sharp left turn, we were soon passing Madame Tussaud's, then walked along the periphery of Regent's Park before veering off in the direction of Camden Town. At this, I began to get an inkling of where we were headed and mentally prepared myself for what I roughly calculated to be a four-mile stroll. Sure enough, we eventually made our way into East Highgate Cemetery, where Holmes soon found the grave of Irene Adler near the Chester Road gate.

I stayed well back, hiding myself behind the thickest oak tree I could find, but peeking around the trunk to keep an eye on Holmes. For a long moment he simply stood there, hands clasped behind his back, staring down at the freshly dug soil. A sudden fear seized me, and I glanced around, hoping that no other visitors would recognize Holmes and wonder why he was standing at an unmarked grave. Questions might be asked, rumors might be started, and we had quite enough on our plate at the moment, thank you very much.

A moment later, Holmes set off at a brisk pace, retracing his steps back towards Baker Street. I dutifully followed behind at a discreet distance, hoping beyond hope that Holmes would return to our rooms, retire for a nap, and then awaken refreshed and a bit more in possession of his faculties. Instead, to my dismay, rather than circling around Regent Park towards Baker Street, Holmes headed straight towards Bloomsbury and a few minutes after that he was ascending the steps into the British Museum. What business he had there was a mystery to me, but I knew that Holmes often made use of their journal and book holdings whenever he wanted to thoroughly research a subject that was new to him.

Once he entered the building I quickly made my way inside, only to find that he had vanished. This would not have been difficult for Holmes to do, as he was as familiar with the British Museum as he was with the major alkaloid poisons. In fact, as I stood there wondering what to do next, it occurred to me that perhaps Holmes had led me here for the express purpose of preventing me from following him any further. If so, he had succeeded wonderfully, but then again, perhaps he was so fixated on his mission that he was completely unaware that I had been trailing after him all this time.

Still, I wasn't completely at a loose end, as Holmes had given me a job to perform; namely, securing the presence of Thomas Edison, Nikola Tesla, and Marie Chartier for his proposed séance tomorrow evening. I felt that his admonition against taking cabs was a little much, but I felt duty-bound to obey his wishes, if for no other reason than I couldn't be sure that Holmes would not simply turn around and begin following me. Based on information I had received from Mycroft Holmes while Holmes lay unconscious on our divan, Edison and Tesla were both still in London seeking financing for their inventions, and of course, their prototypes were still in residence at 221B Baker Street.

The whereabouts of Miss Chartier, on the other hand, were more open to conjecture. Was she still in London? Had she fled the country? Given the situation, there seemed to be only one logical course of action. Both The Langham and The Savoy hotels were approximately a mile or so from the British Museum, so I resolved to visit The Langham first in the hope of finding Edison, then make my way to The Savoy to speak with Tesla. Following that, with no clue whatsoever as to how to find Miss Chartier, I would head to the Diogenes Club to consult with Mycroft Holmes.

Upon approaching the magnificent edifice of The Langham, it warmed my heart to recall that this was where Oscar Wilde and I had enjoyed a rather special and memorable dinner hosted by the American editor J. M. Stoddart many years ago. It was on that very evening that Stoddart had commissioned stories for "Lippincott's Magazine" from both Wilde and I. This gave me the opportunity to write my second Sherlock Holmes novel, "The Sign of the Four," and Wilde eventually produced his memorable, if rather disturbing meditation on art and beauty, "The Picture of Dorian Gray."

On this occasion, upon identifying myself and asking for Thomas Edison, I was escorted to the dining room, where I found the great inventor holed up in a corner rather like an ill-tempered terrier, hiding behind a copy of "The Times." His lunch appeared to consist of nothing more than coffee and apple pie, but he brightened at my appearance and invited me to sit down.

"What news?" Edison asked, with no time for chitchat.

"Holmes is recovered…somewhat," I answered. "At any rate, he's up and about. I just left him at the British Museum."

"Then my device, may I come and retrieve it? Mycroft Holmes vouched for its safety, but I've been worried sick."

"Nothing has been touched," I assured him.

Edison began to get up from the table. "Excellent. Then let's go."

This was a delicate situation. There was no reason Edison shouldn't get his machine back, but I had no intention of relating the full extent of Holmes' suspicions and plans. I most certainly would not tell him that Sherlock Holmes was investigating the murder of Irene Adler, when Edison had witnessed the entire sorry episode himself. Instead, it would be best to say as little as possible, and rely on Edison's own scientific curiosity to encourage him to go along with the plan.

"Actually, we'd like to use it."

"Use my machine?"

"Holmes proposes to hold a séance tomorrow evening in hopes of contacting Miss Adler's spirit."

Edison sank back down into his chair with a look of disbelief. "Seriously? The great, logical, empirical Sherlock Holmes wants to speak with a ghost?"

"He does. And he would like you to be in attendance to witness it. It is, of course, your invention, and if we should have any success it's only right that you should be there."

"Well, of course I'll be there! Why, this is almost ideal! Not to be ghoulish, of course, and Miss Adler's death is a terrible tragedy to be sure, but to try and summon her in the very room in which she died will be the perfect test of my device!"

"Then we'll expect you," I said as I stood up. "Eight o'clock."

"Eight o'clock it is!" Edison stood up as well and we shook hands. "I shall be there!"

As I exited The Langham, I congratulated myself on a job well done. Edison would be in attendance and I had managed to be as discreet as possible regarding Holmes' state of mind and the true purpose of the séance. Now I was faced with what I felt would be the not inconsiderable task of somehow luring Tesla to this same meeting. Edison was one thing, because aside from both his gifts and his ethical failings, he was an eminently practical man. I had approached him in a logical fashion and he had responded precisely as I expected. Tesla was a different case entirely.

There was an air of whimsical unpredictability about him, driven in large part by the simple fact that he was not always inclined to act in his own best interests. If some notion or fancy should seize him, he would pursue it heedless of where it might lead and at what cost. As he himself had expressed it, he needed nor wanted anyone, and with that simple stroke alone had put himself beyond the hopes and fears that push and pull humanity in all directions. Tesla was like a man on a lonely outcropping of rock in the middle of the ocean, his eyes and mind fixated on the universe swirling above him, and oblivious to the foaming fury of the waves crashing all around.

Beyond that, there was little doubt in my mind that witnessing his Death Ray in action must have shaken him to the core. To be sure, his notion that the weapon would lead to universal peace on earth was quite sincere and typical of the man, but unfortunately Tesla's idealism was not to be found in a sizeable percentage of his fellow humans, most especially those in the upper echelons of government and industry. For them, the allure of peace would be dwarfed by the profits to be made from war and conquest, a fact that must have impressed itself firmly on Tesla's mind the moment Marie Chartier pulled the trigger of the Death Ray and unleashed its force against the helpless Miss Adler.

Upon enquiring for Tesla at The Savoy, I was not surprised to learn that he was not in, but took some comfort in learning that he was still a guest of the hotel. London being an excellent place for a man to get lost should he wish to get lost, I saw no point in aimlessly trudging up and down countless lanes and streets searching for a well-dressed Serbian with a thin moustache. Instead, I took a seat in the lobby and settled down to observe the eddies and flows of London's most fashionable citizens while I waited for Tesla to return.

Fashion, I should note, has always fascinated me, steeped as it is in humanity's primordial urge to breed successfully. It may be indelicate of me to say so, but that is the plan and simple truth of the matter, although I suspect few of the dignified guests strolling about looked at it in quite the same light. This collar, that hat, those shoes, and so on, would establish an individual as quite up to the mark and well worth knowing, but the same ensemble next year would be the equivalent of a leper's rags. I felt fortunate indeed to be able to wear my quite comfortable and sensible clothes without subjecting myself to the Procrustean bed of this season's styles.

Still, as I sat there quietly minding my own business, I gradually became aware that I was becoming the object of some attention. Two bellboys had exchanged whispers, a clerk had pointed, and more than a few guests had regarded me as if I were some small rodent that had died and been swept into the gutter. A minute later a gentleman I took to be a manager appeared on the scene. After a moment's consultation with the front desk, he glanced my way, and I could feel a faint prickle of discomfort itching the back of my neck. True, I did not fit in, and The Savoy was an establishment in which fitting in might as well have been the Eleventh Commandment etched in stone, but I was still a perfectly respectable British citizen and I had every right to be there. By now the manager was approaching me with a steady stride and I steeled myself for the confrontation as a well-practised smile made its way across his face.

"Good afternoon, sir," he began. "How are you today?"

"Very well, thank you," I returned.

"Excellent. I am glad to hear it. May I enquire as to your business?"

"I'm waiting for a friend."

"Of course," he answered smoothly. "Your friend's name?"

"Nikola Tesla."

"Ah, Mr. Tesla! And is he expecting you?"

"Not exactly."

"I see. Well, in that event, could I possibly ask you to step outside while you wait?"

As I gazed up at the man I could feel my heart thudding in my chest and as he looked at me with his supercilious smile it was all I could do not to jump up and throttle him then and there. For all of our pretensions, humanity is still an intensely tribal species, and as my appearance marked me as quite evidently not of The Savoy Tribe, I was being politely ejected from the premises. Still, I was here on a mission, and since it wouldn't do to make a scene, I rose and endeavoured to fashion my features into something approaching a smile, but likely managing only a rictus-like grimace. Keeping to his task like a border collie, the manager ushered me not only to the front door, but out of it as well, at which point I turned to him.

"Do you happen to know when Mr. Tesla will return?"

"I'm afraid not, sir."

"Do you have any idea where he has gone?"

"No sir."

Feeling quite strongly that he was lying through his teeth, it finally dawned on me that thanks to a previous case, I had the ultimate trump card to play, and for once it wasn't that I was the friend and colleague of Sherlock Holmes. This was thanks to "The Adventure of the Fallen Soufflé," which had taken Holmes and I into the rarefied air of the British royal family. As noted earlier, I wrote the case up and then consigned it to my despatch box at Cox and Company until such time as its publication would not cause a public furor. Taking the manager gently by the elbow, I leaned towards his ear.

"May I have a quiet word?"

Taking him further away from the entrance of the hotel, I took a glance up and down the street, then lowered my voice as I slid my card into his hand.

"My name is Dr. John Watson, colleague and associate of Sherlock Holmes, the consulting detective. I'm afraid that we do not frequent your establishment on a regular basis; in fact, we do not frequent it at all. However, I believe we have a mutual friend in one of your regular guests—good old Bertie."

As I fully expected, the manager's eyes clouded with confusion, which gave me the opportunity to land the verbal uppercut that I had been aching to deliver physically.

"Oh, I'm sorry, you're clearly not on close terms with him—His Royal Highness."

The manager's eyes went gratifyingly wide in alarm. "King Edward?"

"The very same!" I enthused, before putting my finger to my lips. "Holmes and I were able to render him a small service a short time ago. Lovely fellow! Absolutely mad about Chef Escoffier's chicken stuffed with foie gras as I recall."

"Yes, yes, His Majesty does us the very patronising honour of—I mean, the great honour of patronising our restaurant!" I don't believe I had ever seen beads of sweat form so quickly on a man's forehead as he stumbled on. "Mr. Watson—Dr. Watson! I do beg your pardon, sir. I had no idea that—"

"Now, now," I assured him. "Not to worry. All this is just between us. However, it is absolutely imperative that I get in touch with Mr. Tesla as soon as possible. You're sure you have no idea where he might have gone?"

"Actually, sir, now that I think about it, I believe you'll find him at the Victoria Embankment Gardens. He goes there regularly to feed the pigeons. Our kitchen supplies him with breadcrumbs."

"Excellent!" I enthused. "You have been most helpful, Mr...?"

"Sheffington!"

"Mr. Sheffington, yes. I'll be sure to tell Bertie precisely what sort of fellow you are the next time I see him. Cheerio!" And with a wink and wave I left Mr. Sheffington to ponder my meaning as I headed off.

Quickly locating Tesla in the Victorian Gardens, which stretch for eight city blocks along the banks of the Thames, would be no easy task. Still, I am proud to say that in my time spent living with Sherlock Holmes, some of his habits had rubbed off on me, and so I considered my hunt for Tesla in logical terms. He was there to feed the pigeons breadcrumbs, which they love. What else do pigeons love? Statues.

Bearing this in mind as my one and only clue, within five minutes I had found Tesla sitting on a bench in front of a statue of Scotland's National Poet, the great Robert Burns ("Oor Rab," as he is affectionately styled by the Scots). With pigeons at his feet or jostling for position on the bench next to him, and with one bold fellow atop Tesla's hat, he made quite a spectacle, with other pedestrians making a wide berth. As I approached him, a few of the pigeons fluttered off and Tesla looked up to see me. He shook his head and I could immediately see the great sadness in his eyes.

"Dr. Watson…Dr. Watson…"

My heart immediately went out to the poor fellow and I took a seat next to him, a few of the pigeons graciously consenting to make room for me.

"You can't blame yourself for what happened," I began. "It was terrible and tragic to be sure, but not your fault."

"Wasn't it?" answered Tesla. "Sometimes my ambitions exceed my good sense. It has always been that way with me, and for all of my genius it is a lesson I never seem to learn. Do you know that when I was a young man, I once jumped off a roof with an open umbrella to see if it would soften my fall?"

"And did it?"

"No. With the result that I was confined to bed for two months."

We sat in silence for a moment, and then Tesla gestured towards the birds.

"Pigeons are my friends…my best, and closest, and only friends. I can no longer make any pretence that I understand human beings. And yet, the irony is that if I am fortunate enough to achieve some of my ideals, it would be on behalf of the whole of humanity."

"And you have done that," I offered. "Quite successfully, I might add."

"The reality pales in comparison with my dreams." Tesla paused to look up at the sky. "For example, I hope someday to harness the rays of the sun to operate every machine in our factories, propel every train and automobile, and replace all coal and wood as a producer of heat and electric lighting by using a system of mirrors to heat water into steam to drive turbines. Will I succeed? Perhaps. But then, the scientific man does not aim at an immediate result. My work is like that of the planter—for the future. My duty is to lay the foundation for those who are to come, and point the way."

Unmindful of how rude it might be, I took out my notebook to record these remarkable sentiments of Tesla's as he dumped the last of the breadcrumbs to the ground, sending the pigeons into a feeding frenzy. It was a remarkable thing, that if you had asked me a week ago who was the most gifted inventor and scientist on the planet, I should have unhesitatingly nominated Thomas Edison. But now, beneath the shadow of Robert Burns, there was little question in my mind that I was sitting next to a man who was not merely a genius for the ages, but a humanitarian for the ages as well.

"Shall we go for a walk?" I offered.

Tesla merely nodded and a moment later we were strolling the paths. Holmes had once complimented me on my "great gift of silence," and I employed it now as we walked side by side, each immersed in our own thoughts. After ten minutes or so, Tesla stopped and gazed down at the ground, shaking his head.

"What have I done?"

"What you have always done," I assured him. "You have asked questions and found answers...answers that no one else has ever found before."

"And the longer I live," answered Tesla, "the more I understand there are some questions that should not be asked."

"We are always learning, aren't we?"

"Indeed, Dr. Watson. For when we stop learning, we die."

This was my opportunity, and so I took it, explaining to Tesla that Holmes intended to hold a séance in an effort to contact Irene Adler with Edison's Ghost Machine and that Edison would be there. As I was about to go on at length regarding the importance of his presence, Tesla held up his hand.

"I cannot promise anything. Yes, I want to be there, and I hope to God that Edison's machine works. But to return to the place where Miss Adler was murdered by my own device...I'm not sure I could bear that." Tesla paused to collect himself, then continued. "I did receive a communication from Mycroft Holmes. May I take it that the British government is now in possession of my Death Ray?"

"No. It's still in our rooms. Holmes insisted that everything remain untouched."

"Ah," Tesla nodded, then raised his eyes to the overcast sky, "then I should come. I will try. But please understand that every impression produces a thousand echoes in my mind, so if I should arrive at your doorstep only to turn away, I hope you will forgive me." Tesla paused, and I could tell that there was something else that he was hesitant to say.

"What is it?" I asked.

"Your loyalty and affection for Mr. Holmes are apparent in everything that you say and do. I can only imagine the state of mind that he is in and how concerned you must be. But perhaps some good will come of it all."

"How so?"

"The pressure of occupation and the incessant stream of impressions pouring into our consciousness through all the gateways of knowledge makes modern existence hazardous in many ways. Most people are so absorbed in the contemplation of the outside world that they are wholly oblivious to what is passing on within themselves. But a moment like this, the passing of a loved one, can make the world stop and so give us a reprieve in which to find our true selves. I sincerely hope that is true for Mr. Holmes."

With that, Tesla turned on his heel and I could only watch his tall, slim form recede into the distance as he made his way back in the direction of The Savoy Hotel.

Chapter Nine
A Walking Tour of London

Taking a deep breath and assessing the situation, I determined that I had done all that could be done with Edison and Tesla in terms of summoning them to Holmes' séance. The striking thing about my conversations with both men was, as Holmes might have put it, "the curious incident of the police in the murder case." Namely, there were none. Neither Tesla nor Edison had mentioned any contact with Scotland Yard, and our doorstep had remained mercifully free of Inspectors Lestrade and Gregson. This, clearly, was the invisible hand of Mycroft Holmes at work. It wouldn't do to have Tesla's Death Ray made public knowledge, and so Miss Adler had simply disappeared with no investigation whatsoever. As Miss Chartier had rightly noted, if you are going to commit murder, it's best to kill someone who has been presumed dead for years.

Now all that remained was the problem of Marie Chartier, the final séance attendee upon whose presence Holmes had insisted. The alert reader will note that I approached the task of gathering séance participants in reverse order of difficulty. To begin with, I had a good idea of where I might find Edison and Tesla, but the same could not be said of Miss Chartier. I therefore set out for the Diogenes Club with the view of gaining a private conference with the apparently omniscient and omnipotent Mycroft Holmes.

Upon my first visit to the Diogenes Club some years ago, I will admit that I had been somewhat overawed by the premises and the experience. As a private club, admitting only gentlemen of a very particular sort, and with its "no speaking" rule strictly enforced, it was impressive and eccentric enough that I felt lucky to be allowed inside its hallowed walls. Now, with a few more years under my belt, I had a clearer and somewhat more jaded view of the institution. It was, at its essence, nothing more than a building filled with crotchety old men so compromised by various personality disorders that the prospect of speaking to another human being filled them with horror and rage. They were, to put it mildly, more than slightly ridiculous, but their money and lofty positions entitled them to be catered to like the overtired children they were.

When Mycroft finally appeared to greet me in the Stranger's Room, I quickly caught him up on events. He was relieved, of course, to hear that his younger brother had emerged from his fevered dreams and was out and about in London. He was much less enthused to hear that Holmes was now on the hunt for the murderer of Irene Adler and was planning a séance to try and contact her spirit. Still, being Mycroft Holmes, he had obviously considered what various courses of action his sibling might take upon awakening, and something along those lines had already crossed his mind. I say that because he immediately ticked off half a dozen excellent reasons why the séance should not be allowed. It was all beautifully logical and presented in a most clear and articulate fashion, after which I had a one-word response for Mycroft, which was a simple and emphatic, "No."

True, I had been considerably taken aback when Holmes first proposed the séance, because in all of our time together he had never once evinced the slightest interest in the supernatural; in fact, whenever such a possibility presented itself, as in "The Hound of the Baskervilles," Holmes swept aside the various legends and myths to focus on the very human perpetrator of the crimes being committed in Dartmoor. However, having had time to mull the matter over on my peregrinations around

London, I began to feel that this séance was precisely what Holmes needed. This would be no charade fabricated by a fake medium to relieve the gullible public of a few pounds. This would be a séance conducted under rigorously scientific conditions, and with any luck two of the greatest scientific minds in history would be in attendance.

As for Holmes, the poor man was still in shock from grief, but his mind was such that it simply wouldn't allow him to mourn the loss of Miss Adler. As often happens after the death of a loved one, he was in denial because his mind could not conceive of a world without Miss Adler in it. As a young child I had been compelled to attend a funeral service for a favourite uncle of mine who had suffered an untimely death, and I refused to enter the room to view him in his coffin, fully confident that at any moment he would walk through the front door and lift me up in his arms as he always had.

For Holmes, he couldn't passively accept Miss Adler's death. He had to feel that he was doing something more and this séance was his attempt to do just that. As his friend and colleague, I would make it my business to do everything that he asked to bring the séance about in precisely the way he envisioned, and when Miss Adler ultimately failed to appear or to communicate with us in any way, Holmes would finally have a chance to come to grips with the fact that she would no longer be a part of his life.

As I suspected, Mycroft did have the means to get in touch with Marie Chartier, but as was typical of the man, he refused to tell me how I might find her and that her whereabouts were "government business." This, of course, is a stock phrase typically used by politicians and bureaucrats to keep damaging information from the public and to protect their reputations. In other words, it was arrant nonsense, but in this instance I didn't press the issue, because once Mycroft indicated that he would make certain that Miss Chartier was in attendance, that was all I needed to hear.

I thereupon immediately made my way out of the Diogenes Club and back to Baker Street to see if Holmes had returned. In truth, I didn't expect to find him in residence, and my expectations proved to be quite correct. However, he had been there, as evidenced by the piles of books and journals that were now scattered about our rooms. There was also an envelope with my name on it, and upon opening it found the following note:

> Watson,
>
> Be a good fellow and enquire at Broadstreet & Sons as to a replacement magnifying lens for the one I unfortunately broke. Meet you at Simpson's for dinner at five. No cabs!!!

Normally, of course, I was quite happy to run small errands for Holmes, but in this instance I was keenly aware that Broadstreet & Sons was an emporium on the other side of the city. It was only by leaving that instant and walking at a brisk pace that I would be able to get there and then back to Simpson's to meet Holmes for dinner. Still, dinner at Simpson's with Holmes was such an alluring prospect that I immediately set out, calculating that the exercise of walking across London would give me a sufficient excuse to order anything I liked for dinner, including dessert.

Some time later, with my feet aching, I crossed the threshold of Broadstreet & Sons, and found myself welcomed in by none other than elderly Mr. Broadstreet himself. He greeted me by name, although it had been over a year since either Holmes or I had last been in his shop. When I communicated the nature of my errand, it was no more than thirty seconds later that I had an exact replica of Holmes' broken lens in my hand. Beyond that, the gracious old man refused to take any form of payment. Wrapping it up in paper for me, he simply said, "You tell Mr. Holmes that this is with my compliments."

It was then I recalled the time almost ten years ago that Mr. Broadstreet's then teenage daughter had disappeared under the influence of a disreputable young Duke, and it was Holmes who had returned her to her frantic father, with the Duke suitably shaken by the quiet word I had seen Holmes whisper in his ear. No, it wasn't an adventure suitable for writing up in "The Strand," but it was one of the countless instances in which Holmes had rendered his services to desperate people who had nowhere else to turn, and one more example of why London needed Sherlock Holmes at his very best.

With Holmes' new lens in my pocket, and feeling more than a bit peckish after my exertions of the afternoon, I made my way to Simpson's-in-the-Strand for a well-deserved dinner. Should the reader not have had the pleasure of dining at Simpson's, rest assured, it was in my humble estimation, the finest restaurant in the world. Not only was the quality of their roasts utterly unsurpassed, but one was not required to dress up like a fashionable toff to enter the premises, and once you paid your half crown, the waiters would continue to bring you food until you begged for mercy.

I began with a drink as I waited for Holmes, and when five o'clock came and went, I finally ordered, knowing that Holmes wouldn't mind and assuming he was caught up in business elsewhere. With an eye on the door, I kept waiting and kept eating, until it was apparent that Holmes would not be joining me. And so, perhaps two hours later, filled to the brim with roast beef, horseradish sauce, and claret, I lurched back out onto the streets as best as I was able. By now, night had fallen, and while under normal circumstances I might have enjoyed the stroll back to Baker Street to aid in my digestion, upon this occasion I found that I wasn't able to stand quite as erectly as I wished thanks to the rather distended condition of my stomach.

This was a predicament that I had not anticipated, as Holmes had expressly forbidden the use of any cabs. Standing near the street, with one empty cab after another whistling by, I decided to apply pure logic to the situation. If Holmes had joined me for dinner, no doubt we would have shared a cab back to Baker Street. That was all the logic that I needed. Hailing a cab, I somehow negotiated myself inside, then sat back for the ride home.

Disembarking outside 221B, a glance upwards showed that a light was on, so perhaps Holmes had returned, or perhaps he had returned and then gone out again. Quietly making my way up our stairs so as not to disturb Holmes if he were in, I opened our door slowly and listened. Immediately, I heard the sound of deep, heavy breathing. Venturing further inside, the first thing I observed was that even more books and journals had been flung everywhere, and there was Holmes himself, fast asleep on the divan, his fingers stuck between the pages of one of the journals.

"Is that you, my love?"

Admittedly, this was not the greeting I expected to hear from Holmes, but I quickly discerned that the question was not directed at me; but rather, to Miss Adler who was, presumably, inhabiting Holmes' dreams as he was still fast asleep. As silently as possible, I made my way to the armchair and sat down to observe my friend. With his pale, drawn face, whatever he had been up to during the day had put an undue strain upon his system, and the worst of it was that even now, what sleep he could find was far from restful. His eyes were constantly moving, his lips muttering incomprehensible syllables as he tossed and turned.

I brought out my notebook to have it ready should Holmes happen to say anything of importance, then picked up the novel that Miss Adler had been reading—"The Awakening," by the American author Kate Chopin. I opened it to the first page, seeing the passage that Tesla had committed to memory with only a glance, and the next thing I knew I awoke with a jolt at a shout from Holmes.

"I can't make bricks without clay!"

"No, I suppose not," I answered, not even sure an answer was required. Fumbling for my pocket watch, I was disconcerted to see that it was now after midnight. Holmes looked at me bleary-eyed, clearly having just awoken.

"Oh, hello Watson. I didn't see you there. I just had the most remarkable dream."

"Involving Miss Adler, I presume."

Suspicion immediately clouded Holmes' eyes. "How on earth did you know that?"

"You were speaking to her."

"And what did I say?"

"I'm sure I don't know. It was all so much mumbling as best I could make out."

"Yes, well, she has been helping me with the case. She is here, Watson, whether in disembodied form in this room or only in my heart I cannot tell, but she agrees that there is a conspiracy, webs of lies and deceit engulfed in the white fire of hundreds of thousands of volts, but the trouble is we're an inch off. There are three essential clues, and of course three divided by three equals one truth, and that is what we are searching for." Holmes paused in his ravings to look at me searchingly. "Stand up."

Anxious to not distress him any further, I immediately did his bidding as he stood up as well.

"Excellent," he said, and then indicated the divan. "Now lie down."

"What are we doing?" I asked.

"Isn't it obvious? You shall be me and I shall be you. Please."

As I lay down on the divan, Holmes took out his pocket watch, then held my wrist, checking my pulse.

"There we are. Yes, this was the scene precisely. After going into shock following Irene's death, I have just awoken and you are checking my pulse. And do you remember what you said to me? What were your first words?"

Casting my mind back as best I was able, I tried to conjure up the scene from memory and to my relief it came rushing back to me.

"'Finally. Thank God'"

"Exactly! Because I had been gone for three days! You see the significance? How many days was Jesus Christ entombed before his Resurrection? And what is the number that obsesses Nikola Tesla? The number three! There, you see? Hardly a coincidence."

Anxious to divert Holmes from this nonsensical line of thought, I pointed at the journal he had just set aside before checking my pulse.

"What is it you have there, Holmes?"

"Data!" Holmes picked the journal up and waved it in the air. "Data, data, data. I cannot make bricks without clay!"

Just when I was afraid that we were right back where we started, Holmes began to pace up and down and talk a trifle more lucidly.

"I have been immersing myself in the scientific articles of Mr. Tesla. They're brilliant...the sheer scope of his ideas is absolutely breathtaking. He talks about getting energy from the sun, controlling the weather, remote controlled machines, and claims that small vest-pocket instruments will be our telephones, and that newspapers will be printed in our homes overnight. He is a modern Prometheus, seeking to give mankind gifts for which we are not yet ready. But most strikingly, do you know what his writings are filled with?"

"Calculations?" I guessed.

"Love. Tesla is a man filled with love, Watson."

"But how can that be?" I answered. "You heard him yourself. He doesn't love or want or need anyone. He wraps himself up in his cloak of genius and keeps the rest of humanity at a distance to focus on his work."

"True. Tesla doesn't love anything so insubstantial as another human being. But if you recall, he told us that electricity is his mistress."

"Whatever that means."

"It means that for Tesla, it is the vital fluid! Like the blood in our veins, electricity is the elixir of the universe! And what is the universe? It is a symphony of waves and vibrations! And yet, the energy of a single thought may determine the motion of a universe. Don't you see?" Holmes opened the journal and pointed to an article. "It's all here in his own words! For Tesla, there is no such thing as individuality. Every person is but a wave passing through space, ever-changing from minute to minute as we travel along into and then out of our lives. Listen to this..." Holmes began reading from the journal:

> "We are held together, like the stars in the heavens, with ties inseparable. These ties we cannot see, but we can feel them. I cut my finger and it pains me: This finger is a part of me. I see my friend hurt and it hurts me too: My friend and I are one. And now I see stricken down an enemy, a lump of matter which, of all lumps of matter in the universe, I care least for, and it still grieves me. Does this not prove that each of us is only part of a whole?"

Flinging the journal aside, Holmes walked to our window and gazed out into the night. "Tesla has seen the truth...the one great truth. We are all one, Watson. The individual is ephemeral, races and nations come and pass away, but humanity and love remain..."

As Holmes buried his face in his hands, I raked my mind for something to say to him, something of comfort and wisdom to try and ease the agony of his grief, but all I could manage was, "Holmes...you really must rest."

"And I shall. We will all rest soon enough, our waves stilled into silence..." With his back turned to me, I couldn't be certain, but he appeared to wipe away a tear. However, when he turned towards me, his face was set with a look of resolution. "But now to the business at hand. Have you my new lens?"

"Yes!" I had quite forgotten it, but pulled the paper package from my pocket and handed it to Holmes. He immediately unwrapped it, examining the lens closely.

"Excellent! Most excellent! Old Broadstreet knows his business, to be sure. Now then..." Holmes hesitated, then looked at me. "Oh dear. A thousand apologies, Watson! I neglected to join you for dinner!"

"No matter," I assured him. "I assumed you were busy."

"And I was! Indeed I was! Still, that's a poor excuse for my behaviour. I shall make it up to you once this case is finished. Will you allow me to do that?"

"Of course! Please don't worry yourself. The roast beef was delicious, with or without your company."

"Capital! I do appreciate the sense of perspective you bring to things, Watson. Now then, on to our final and most important piece of business. Have you arranged this evening's séance?"

"About that," I began, not sure quite how to convey to Holmes that all of his requested participants might not be in attendance. "Edison is quite happy to come because he wants to try and contact Miss Adler with his machine. Miss Chartier, on the other hand, has completely disappeared—"

"Naturally enough," interrupted Holmes. "She fears that she will be charged with murder."

"But I have your brother's assurance that he knows where she is and that she will be here."

"Of course he knows her whereabouts!" enthused Holmes. "He is Mycroft, after all! No doubt he has his best agents constantly on her trail. Not a bad policy at all, although perhaps more dangerous than his agents realise. And Tesla?"

"I believe he will come, but I can't be sure. You met the man, Holmes. He's in a different world from us."

"Indeed he is. Poor fellow...poor, poor fellow. So far ahead of his time that he's mistaken for a mad dreamer. I imagine he's rethinking the whole premise of his Death Ray and the notion that an ultimate weapon will lead to ultimate peace. But we need him here, and I will require his services before the séance, so that settles it..."

"Settles what?"

"I'm off."

Striding to our coat stand, Holmes stood in front of it for a long moment, then reached for his Inverness and deerstalker. He turned to me and no doubt perceived the dubious and concerned expression on my face. "Yes, Watson, I know. Inappropriate attire for the city. But perhaps if I look like Sherlock Holmes, it will help me feel like Sherlock Holmes. At least, let's hope so."

"Where are you going?" I asked.

"To speak with Tesla."

"At this hour?"

"I have learned a great deal about our friend Tesla. Apparently, he rarely sleeps. His mind is too filled with ideas."

"Then you're going to The Savoy Hotel?"

"Unless you know better. Has he moved hotels?"

"No, but you might have better luck finding him in the Victoria Embankment Gardens near the statue of Robert Burns. He has a special affinity for pigeons, apparently. Electricity may be his mistress, but it is the pigeons who are his friends."

"Good old Watson!" Holmes even managed a smile. "Well done, old friend!"

"But Holmes..."

"Yes? What is it? I'm troubling you."

"May I be frank?"

"Please."

"It's almost one o'clock in the morning, you're consulting with your dead lover regarding her murder in your dreams, and now you're going to the park to talk to a mad scientist as he feeds his friends the pigeons."

"I see. You think I'm raving. You fear for my mental stability." Holmes came back towards me, a wild look in his eyes. "Have you been in touch with your colleague Dr. Phelps again? Is that what's going on here?"

Holmes rushed to the window, looking out into the darkness in a panic. "Is there a carriage coming to take me to Bartholomew's Hospital for observation? Tell me the truth, Watson!"

"Holmes, I promise that no one is coming for you! But you're distraught...grieving. Your mind is looking for answers, but the reality of the human condition is that sometimes there are no answers. Terrible, unthinkable things happen for no reason."

"True...indisputably true. And yet...why is everything one inch off?"

"I don't know what you mean by that."

"Neither do I. I just know that something's wrong... something's amiss...it's not making sense...I can't make sense of it! And that's my job! To make sense of the world! To explain things! That is the meaning of my existence, the pursuit to which I have devoted my life, but now...now I can't trust my own senses! I can't trust anything or anyone! There's a conspiracy, but it's so large that it envelops everything, and I can't seem to claw my way to the edge of it to see it for what it is...I feel as if I'm lost in a dream...a nightmare, of someone else's devising."

"Holmes, people create conspiracies when their reality is so horrible they simply can't accept what has happened. Forty years ago a theatre full of people watched John Wilkes Booth assassinate Abraham Lincoln, and yet within days there were theories saying the Pope was responsible."

"Then what should I do?"

"First, you need a decent night's sleep. And you must allow yourself to grieve. It will take time. And then, eventually, we'll take on a new case or two...and you can become Sherlock Holmes again, which is what London needs. What the world needs. And most importantly, it's what you need...not this ghost-hunting business."

"Aren't we always hunting ghosts?" answered Holmes. "In our dreams...in our memories. Searching for people who are no longer with us...seeking to be with them once again. There is a seed within humanity that makes us hope and yearn for a life beyond this. And it takes but the smallest drop of water, the barest possibility of hope, for that belief to spring to full flower in an instant. There is nothing that we desire more than for our existence to transcend these temporary, shadow lives that we lead. And so we imagine endless time in an endless universe of which we are a part, as is everyone we have ever loved. What do you say, Watson? Speaking as a medical man, as someone who has seen more than his fair share of death, do you believe that ghosts exist?"

"I don't know," I replied. "What I do believe is that exceptional claims require exceptional proof."

Holmes began to circle me, eyeing me up and down before finally stopping in front of me.

"That's excellent. Carry that uncertainty with you always. Do not fear it, for uncertainty is the only thing that is certain. For example, how do I know I can trust you? As my friend for many years, I know that is a terrible thing to say, but how do I know anything when I know nothing? I have been cast back on myself and only myself. My own senses, my own deductive faculties...if I can trust even those. If I don't know what reality is, then I must create my own...and use my reality to crack the illusion within which I am living...or go mad in the attempt."

Taking hold of the fabric of my lapel, Holmes felt it and then ran his fingers across my cheek, his eyes boring into mine.

"I believe you are Watson. I believe you are my friend. You sleep. Sleep for both of us. I need to see Tesla. And the séance must take place tonight with all of us present. I don't propose to torment you or myself any longer. The séance will reveal whatever truth or lies there may be in the world, and I shall simply have to live with the consequences..."

And with that, Holmes was gone.

Chapter Ten
Preparations for a Séance

I briefly flirted with the idea of trying to follow Holmes, but if I had failed in that during the day, I most certainly had no chance of succeeding at this hour. Besides, Holmes was not a man who could be followed if he did not want to be followed. Instead, there seemed to be only one sensible course of action, which was to take myself to bed and prepare for what was bound to be a momentous day ahead. I imagined that I would be able to fall asleep quickly, but just as I could feel myself drifting off, some vision or word from the past few days would lurch into my consciousness, and I would find myself fully awake again, the same thoughts cycling through my head over and over. At what time I finally succumbed to exhaustion I have no idea, but when I awoke, it took me some time to orient myself.

Checking my watch, I was startled to find that it was already nine in the morning and immediately scrambled out of bed. Holmes was still out doing God knows what, but I could see from the derangement of our rooms that he had returned at some point while I was still asleep. Considering the fact that Holmes' séance was several hours off and that I had no immediate duties to attend to, I made the pragmatic decision to treat myself like a civilised human being. Bathing and shaving, I changed clothes and sat down to a simple meal of sausages, eggs, and toast. Suitably fortified, I made some effort at tidying the place up, with frequent glances out the window for Holmes.

Trying to create some order out of the dozens of books and scientific journals Holmes had somehow procured, I began to glance through them, and they ranged from mind-numbingly detailed articles on gasoline-powered engines to designs for different types of aircraft. Here and there I found Tesla's work, but confess that I could barely make heads or tails of it. His obsession with energy and waves was evident, even detailing in one article how he had almost brought down a steel-girder building by simply tapping at a metal beam at such precise intervals that the vibrations steadily built up until the entire structure was trembling as if in an earthquake.

My research was interrupted by the ringing of our bell, and when I went downstairs a messenger handed me an envelope.

"Telegram for Dr. John Watson, sir."

Opening it, I saw immediately that it was from Holmes, and the few words it contained froze the blood in my veins.

>MORIARTY IS ALIVE.
>ON HIS TRAIL.
>CONSPIRACY UNRAVELLING.
>MEET ME AT LIVERPOOL LIME STREET STATION.
>HURRY!

Rushing back upstairs to retrieve my coat, it was everything I could do to swallow down the panic that was threatening to envelop me. Holmes had clearly cracked under the strain of the past few days and had somehow wound up in Liverpool of all places. Making my way to Marylebone Station as quickly as I could, I was soon on the train heading north to Merseyside. Relieved to have a compartment to myself, I sat down to compose my scattered thoughts. What had sent Holmes spinning down this rabbit hole?

Was it the presence of Moriarty's daughter, Marie Chartier? Was there any possibility that Professor Moriarty was somehow still alive? After all, I had never seen his broken corpse at the bottom of the Reichenbach Falls and only had Holmes' word regarding what had happened there. More likely was the fact that in his grief, his mind weaving one conspiracy after another, Holmes had concluded that only his mortal enemy could be responsible for the death of Irene Adler, and so Moriarty had been resurrected, not in real life, but in the mind of Sherlock Holmes.

Then there was the issue of time and Holmes' séance at eight o'clock that evening, if in fact he still planned on conducting a séance. The journey from London to Liverpool would take nearly four hours, and if I could find Holmes quickly at the station, then we could get back on the return train to London and make it to Baker Street in time to receive our guests. Who might actually be in attendance? There was no telling where Tesla might end up, and if there was ever a human enigma, it was Marie Chartier, whose motives and actions were never entirely predictable. For all I knew Mycroft Holmes might put in an appearance, and if I couldn't locate Holmes at the Liverpool Station it might just be Edison and I.

Checking the mileposts against my watch, I determined that the express train was hurtling up the London & North Western line at a respectable 56 MPH, but by the time we reached Liverpool Station it seemed as if an eternity had passed. I burst from the carriage and looked up and down the platform, hoping beyond hope that I would see Holmes' deerstalker standing out in the crowd. If Holmes was here he would surely be looking out for me, and he was a hard man to miss, but there was no sign of him at all. Had he ever been here in the first place? Where was he now? Checking the ticket booths with no success, I was approached by a railway porter.

"Can I help you, sir?"

"I'm looking for Sherlock Holmes," I replied.

"I believe you'll find him in London, sir. 221B Baker Street is the address."

"I believe you are correct," I answered. "You're familiar with the stories, I take it?"

"I should say so, sir! Well, the good ones at any rate. 'The Hound of the Baskervilles?' Masterful. But that terrible one last year, what was it, 'The Adventure of the Golden Pince-Nez?' My God. I told the wife I could write something better than that rubbish any day of the week."

"Did you?" I replied, feeling myself getting a trifle warm under the collar.

"Were you wanting to go to London, sir? If you hurry, you'll just be able to catch the train."

Sure enough, I could see that the return train was starting to build up steam, and it was only with an unseemly liveliness for a man of my age that I was able to board the train at the very last moment. As I sat back in my seat for the return journey, I attempted to put the porter's literary critique out of my head and give myself up to whatever events might soon unfold. There were an untold number of questions to be asked, but no way of ascertaining the answers as the train built up speed out of Liverpool.

Given that, I turned my gaze out the window and remembered the occasion when Holmes and I had been sharing a carriage and I made an offhand remark regarding the peaceful English countryside through which we were passing. To this day, I can remember Holmes' response, "Think of the deeds of hellish cruelty, the hidden wickedness which may go on, year in, year out, in such places, and none the wiser." It was easy to forget that was the world in which Sherlock Holmes was almost perpetually immersed. Even if no tragic or horrible case had been brought to our attention, Holmes was constantly aware of the evils that human beings were inflicting upon one another. No wonder that he finally sought refuge in the safe and sane harbor of Miss Adler, and no wonder that her absence had deranged his senses.

Given the gentle, rhythmic swaying of the carriage upon the rails, I must have nodded off at some point, for it was only the screeching sound of the brakes as we pulled into Marylebone Station that brought me back to my senses. Checking my watch, I saw that I had just enough time to make it to Baker Street by eight o'clock. As I hurried along, I heard the sound of thunder in the distance, then observed a stooped, shuffling figure up ahead of me. Quickening my pace, I soon caught up with Thomas Edison, who was delighted to see me.

"A momentous day for mankind, Dr. Watson!" he began. "We shall see if death can be overcome...if our existence transcends our passing. We are about to witness history!"

As touched as I was by his almost childish enthusiasm, it was an enthusiasm I did not share. I was too worried about where Holmes might be and what state of mind he might be in. However, I did not communicate this to Edison, and instead diverted the conversation to some of his other inventions, which he was quite delighted to expound upon at length. Regardless of the invention, I was assured that the essence of it was his and his alone, and that without his hard work and genius, devices such as the telephone, telegraph, and phonograph would be mere curiosities with no practical benefit and no profit to be made. To my amusement, he bemoaned the first patent that he received at the age of twenty-two for an electric vote recorder for elections, not realising there was no market for a machine that would accurately tally votes and make changing the results impossible.

I was interested to hear his thoughts on motion pictures, which I had first witnessed at the Empire Theatre of the Varieties in Leicester Square some years earlier. To Edison's mind, they were useful in terms of their ability to tempt pennies from the poor, the ignorant, and the immigrants, but he lamented the fact that anyone with a camera could make a movie, which made it difficult to monopolize the industry. He then proceeded to launch into his opinion regarding society in general, which, predictably enough, was not a particularly glowing assessment.

After a diatribe lasting several city blocks, he finally concluded by saying, "And I will tell you the problem with the modern world, Dr. Watson. Opportunity is missed by most people because it is dressed in overalls and looks like work. That, my good sir, is the long and short of it."

Thankfully, by this point we were now on Baker Street, and as we approached 221B, to my considerable relief I saw Tesla standing motionless outside the door holding what appeared to be a large hatbox in his hands. He had decided to come after all, but now, apparently, faced with the prospect of going inside, he was having second thoughts.

"Mr. Tesla!" I said as I approached him. "How very good of you to come."

"Perhaps..." Tesla held out the box. "...you could give this to Mr. Holmes. Considering the tragedy that I caused, I really should not be here."

"Nonsense! Holmes wants you here. I would go so far as to say that he needs you here, Mr. Tesla. Please."

As Tesla hesitated, Edison couldn't stop himself from having a jab at his old foe.

"Never mind, Dr. Watson. Clearly, Tesla doesn't want to witness the single greatest invention in history come to life for the simple reason that it's not his. His ego couldn't stand it."

Tesla turned his blue eyes on Edison, and I would swear there was pity in them. "Should your device work, I would be most happy for you, Edison. I do not think there is any thrill that can go through the human heart like that felt by the inventor as he sees some creation of his brain unfolding to success. Such emotions make a man forget food, sleep, friends, love, everything." As another rumble of thunder sounded to the east, Tesla looked in that direction and smiled. "That is a good sign. I was born in the midst of a torrential deluge and have always considered myself a child of the storm. Let us proceed, Dr. Watson."

Not wishing to give Tesla the chance to change his mind, I swiftly opened the door and herded both men up the stairs. As we entered our rooms, I was desperately hoping to see Holmes waiting for us, but he was nowhere to be seen. Tesla and Edison, meanwhile, made straight for their respective inventions. Setting down the mysterious box he had brought with him, Tesla picked up his Death Ray and stared at it, shaking his head at the destruction it had wrought, while Edison closely examined every inch of his Ghost Machine.

"Yes, yes, perfectly intact!" said Edison. "I was worried that Morgan might have bought Holmes off and we would arrive to find both of our inventions missing."

It had been a long day, and I turned on Edison, my temper instantly flaring up. "Sherlock Holmes cannot be bought off! He is not some corporate criminal with a vacuum where his conscience ought to be! Is that understood?"

Edison had the good grace to appear at least slightly abashed as Tesla gazed around the room.

"But Mr. Holmes, he is not here?"

"Apparently not," I answered. After a moment's hesitation, I felt obliged to divulge just a trifle more to Tesla and Edison in case the events of the evening should drift into even stranger territory than I imagined they would. "Gentlemen, there is something I must tell you in confidence. Holmes is not quite himself. His ideas and activities have been somewhat erratic. I have no doubt that he will arrive soon, but I'm not entirely sure what to expect when he does."

"Mr. Holmes has suffered a great loss," offered Tesla. "It is only natural that his mind should be in some disorder, and every man of artistic temperament has relapsed from the great enthusiasms that buoy him up and sweep him forward. In time, no doubt he will recover."

It was only then that I spotted an envelope with my name it. Almost afraid to open it for fear of what it might contain, I was considerably relieved to find that it was simply a short note from Holmes and a diagram of how he wished the furniture in the room to be arranged for the séance. This heartened me slightly—as it indicated that Holmes was still thinking somewhat clearly and that he would be back very shortly.

"Gentlemen," I turned to Tesla and Edison, "Holmes has left explicit instructions as to how he wants the room and furniture arranged. Could I possibly impose upon you to assist me?"

"Of course!" responded Edison enthusiastically. "I can't speak for our visionary friend here, but there's nothing I enjoy more than plain, simple, hard work."

"I would be most happy to assist," added Tesla, brushing Edison's veiled insult aside.

"Excellent! Then Mr. Tesla, if you would be so kind as to help me move that table and four chairs over here, we will let Mr. Edison place his Ghost Machine into what he feels is the best position."

As we all set to our respective tasks, gentle drops of rain began to patter against the window, and Edison returned to the theme that seemed to obsess him; namely, how he worked harder than anyone else in the world.

"In fact, speaking of work, Dr. Watson, when I'm in my laboratory, I put in eighteen to twenty hours every day, and let me tell you this, not one of my inventions came by accident. I see a worthwhile need to be met and I make trial after trial until the answer comes. What it boils down to is one percent inspiration and ninety-nine percent perspiration."

"Surely you're exaggerating," I answered.

"Not at all." To my surprise, Tesla had chimed in. "Every word he says is true."

Edison stared at Tesla in shock, genuinely taken aback. "Why, thank you, Nikola! That's damned decent of you!"

"I worked with Edison for a year," Tesla continued, "and if he had to find a needle in a haystack, he would proceed at once with the diligence of a bee to examine straw after straw until he found the object of his search. I was a sorry witness to such doings, knowing that a little theory and calculation would have saved him ninety percent of his labour. His method is inefficient in the extreme."

"Pah! Rubbish! Say what you want about my method, Tesla, but it works."

"Then presumably your method is somewhat different, Mr. Tesla?" I asked.

"Quite so." Tesla placed a chair next to the table and sat down, crossing his legs with elegant ease. "For me, instinct is something that transcends knowledge, and I see my inventions in visions. I have never needed models, drawings, or experiments because my memory is three-dimensional. I simply visualise what it is I want to create and I am able to develop and perfect a conception without touching anything. I build it in my imagination. It is absolutely immaterial to me whether I run a turbine in my mind or test it in my shop."

This claim appeared to incense Edison to no end. "Oh, for the love of—do you seriously expect anyone to believe that claptrap?"

"For example," Tesla went on, "when I was twenty-four years old and working in Budapest, a vision of the alternating current induction motor simply came to me—a motor that would do the work of the world and be in harmony with nature, by simply utilising rotating magnetic fields."

"Poppycock!" shouted Edison. "That's sheer poppycock!"

"What exactly happened, Mr. Tesla?" I asked.

"Well, to clarify, the general notion of my motor had been on my mind for some time, especially once I realised how inefficient and impractical Edison's direct current system was. So, whether I was out for a walk, dining, or feeding my pigeon friends, the concept of a motor driven by alternating current was always ticking steadily away in some corner of my mind, despite the best and brightest minds in electricity telling me that it was impossible. Then one afternoon, which is ever present in my recollection, I was enjoying a walk with my friend Anthony Szigeti in Varosliget Park and reciting poetry. At that age I knew entire works by heart, word for word. One of these was

Goethe's 'Faust.' The sun was just setting and it reminded me of a glorious passage:

>'The glow retreats, done is the day of toil
>It yonder hastes, new fields of life exploring
>Ah, that no wing can lift me from the soil
>Upon its track to follow, follow soaring!'

"As I uttered those inspiring words the idea came like a flash of lightning and in an instant the truth was revealed. I cannot begin to describe my emotions. I instantly drew with a stick in the sand the image that had appeared in my mind, and I will tell you that Pygmalion seeing his statue come to life could not have been more deeply moved. It was this simple diagram that I subsequently used in my address before the American Institute of Electrical Engineers, and thus, it was in that very moment that Mr. Edison's direct current electrical system was consigned to the dustbin of history."

It was a stunning, beautiful, poetic story, and it was all I could do not to burst into spontaneous applause. Instead, I simply shook my head in awe at the capacities of the human mind, and even more particularly, of Tesla's mind. "Amazing, Mr. Tesla! Quite wonderful!"

Turning to observe Edison's reaction to Tesla's recollection, he was glowering at nothing in particular, with his jaw clenched and his fists coiled up into balls as a more steady rain began to fall outside.

"I hate him," announced Edison.

Just as I began to fear that a new, and rather physical chapter was about to be added to the rivalry between Tesla and Edison, we all became aware that Holmes was now in the room. At some point in all the activity he had emerged silently from his bedroom, and as he looked around at our preparations, I observed that he was immaculately groomed and dressed, and appeared not only well rested, but almost serene. A thousand questions immediately ran through my mind, but they would have to wait as Holmes spread his arms in welcome.

"Gentlemen, you have outdone yourselves! Excellent! Everything is in readiness." He turned in my direction. "Watson, I shall make profuse apologies to you on a number of counts at the very first opportunity, but as you are well aware, my mind has been in some degree of disarray of late."

Holmes' attention was then drawn to the table, which was now in the centre of the room, surrounded by four chairs.

"But what's this? We need one more chair!" He ticked the names off on his fingers. "Holmes, Watson, Edison, Tesla, and Marie Chartier. That's five people and I see only four chairs."

"You don't seriously expect Miss Chartier to be here?" asked Tesla incredulously.

"Why on earth not?" answered Holmes.

"Because we watched her murder Irene Adler!" exclaimed Edison.

"Oh that." Holmes retrieved another chair and placed it at the table. "Merely the climax of the conspiracy. She'll be here."

"What's that?" Edison was like a fox who has just heard the cry of a hound in the distance. "Conspiracy? What conspiracy? Is it Morgan and his damned lawyers again? You see, Dr. Watson? I knew it! He's after my invention!"

Even the word "conspiracy" is like a contagion to inventors, who live in constant fear of their life's work being stolen, and Tesla immediately joined in the hue and cry. "And mine as well, no doubt! Perhaps Morgan and the German government have joined forces to steal my Death Ray!"

"Please calm yourselves, gentlemen," soothed Holmes. "The avarice of J. P. Morgan, considerable as it may be, is not inspired by any particular genius. Nor is the German government involved. No, in this case we have been moved, all of us, like chess pieces by a truly transcendent intellect. And the clearer it becomes to me, the more I stand in awe of both its intricacy and its simplicity."

"But if there is a conspiracy, who is behind it?" cried Edison.

"Yes, who?" added Tesla.

I stared at Holmes, my heart in my throat, praying that he wouldn't lay recent events at the feet of Professor Moriarty and reveal to Tesla and Edison just how deranged his thoughts had become. But before Holmes could say another word, our door opened and Marie Chartier entered the room. Holding a damp umbrella in one hand, she kept one arm behind her back as she closed the door and stepped towards us.

"I am here at the request of the British government," she began. "And I warn you, I am armed." As if any proof of that was needed, she then pointed what I instantly recognised as a German Mauser towards us. Should the reader not be familiar, the Mauser is a particularly ugly weapon, capable of inflicting even uglier wounds, and the fact that Miss Chartier was holding a German pistol in her hand only served to confirm her dealings with the German government. As Edison and Tesla instinctively held up their hands, Holmes offered Miss Chartier a broad smile.

"Well, of course you are! How lovely to see you again, my dear. Should you fear for a moment for your life or freedom, by all means blast away to your heart's content!"

"I say, Holmes!" I objected, dismayed at his rather cavalier attitude.

"Personally, I would prefer not to be shot," said Tesla.

"And you won't be," assured Holmes. "Please make yourself comfortable, Miss Chartier. Have you brought the device I requested, Mr. Tesla?"

I had completely forgotten about Tesla's mystery box, but now he retrieved it and handed it to Holmes. "It is here."

"Wonderful!" Holmes proceeded to open the box and removed from it one of the strangest devices I have ever seen in my life. Sitting atop a wooden base, a thick cylinder was wrapped entirely around with copper wire, and on top of the cylinder was a silver ball fabricated from some kind of metal. Its very appearance sent a shiver of ominous foreboding through me.

"What in God's name is it?" I asked.

"A Tesla coil," answered Holmes. "Named after our friend here, who invented it in 1891. Would you care to explain its purpose, Mr. Tesla?"

"But of course. It is an electrical resonant transformer circuit, used to produce high-voltage, low-current, high-frequency electricity. I use it for my experiments in lighting, phosphorescence, and wireless electricity."

"But why do we need it?" I asked. "What is it for?"

"This is our signal!" enthused Holmes. "Our beacon to the bioelectrical remains of Irene Adler! It is my theory that a strong electrical field will be required to draw her essence towards us and Mr. Edison's Ghost Machine. Merely a theory, of course, but a theory that we will now have the luxury of putting to the test. So, now that we are all gathered, let us begin our séance. If everyone would be so kind as to sit around the table, we shall commence our efforts to communicate with the realm beyond."

Chapter Eleven
The Scientific Séance

Slowly, we all took our seats, even Miss Chartier, with her hand still on her gun. Holmes flipped the switch to activate Edison's Ghost Machine, then set the Tesla coil in the middle of the table. With the rest of us seated, he proceeded to extinguish the lights, leaving only the faintest glow from the streetlights coming through the windows. He then joined us at the table as the storm outside continued to build. While I had no expectations whatsoever of any spectres materialising through the walls to join us, I must say that I found the situation and the ambience of the room somewhat unsettling. The only thing to do was indulge Holmes' whim, let him get it out of his system, and then gradually help him resume his life as the world's premier consulting detective, if such a thing were even possible.

"Mr. Tesla," Holmes began, "how long will the battery for your Tesla coil last?"

"It is fully charged and should last up to an hour."

"More than enough time for our purposes," said Holmes. "Would you please be so kind as to activate the device?"

Tesla reached for a switch, and as he touched it, the Tesla coil came to life with a low hum. There was a crackle of electricity as sparks flew around the top of the metal orb and the room was filled with an unsettling blue light. The device itself was mesmerising, drawing our full attention with its unearthly beauty, and helping me to realise why Tesla regarded electricity as a living thing.

"Then we are ready to begin," said Holmes. "Will you all join hands, please?"

Looking to our left and right, we all clasped hands, even Miss Chartier, who carefully put the Mauser on the table in front of her. I found myself holding her hand on my right, and Edison's hand on my left, while Holmes held Miss Chartier's right hand and Tesla's left hand. Even as the Tesla coil sparked and crackled before us, an answering spark and crackle of lightning outside answered, almost as if the forces of electricity were conspiring to have a conversation between them that we mere humans would never understand.

Holmes looked around the table. "As you all know, we have convened here together for one purpose and one purpose alone—to summon the departed Irene Adler once more into our presence. She was...is...the most remarkable woman I have ever known. If there is any spirit, any bioelectrical form that can transcend death and return to speak to us, it is her. Of that, I am certain. And so we must now open the valve between worlds, focus our thoughts and energies, and open our minds to both the possible and the impossible."

Holmes paused and then closed his eyes. I could feel Miss Chartier's hand squeezing mine tighter as my heart began to thud heavily in my chest. This was all for naught, I knew that, for there were no such things as ghosts and spirits, and yet I was becoming more and more unnerved just the same.

"Irene...are you here?" began Holmes. "Can you join us? If so, please give us a sign."

"Holmes," I interrupted. "Come now. This is ridiculous."

"Is it?" Holmes opened his eyes. "Why is it ridiculous to try to breach the gap between the dead and the living—to prove what humanity has always sought to prove—that our existence transcends our brief time on this mortal coil, and that a spark of immortality exists within each of us...but we need some sign.

Can you hear me, Irene? Can you give us some sign of your presence?"

And as I looked sideways at Miss Chartier to see her reaction to all this, a book fell off one of the shelves and clattered to the floor.

"My God!" cried Tesla as I felt Edison's hand practically crushing my fingers in his excitement.

Two more books tumbled to the floor, one after the other.

"Marvellous, my dear!" cried Holmes. "So you are here? It is you! It is you, isn't it, Irene? Show yourself to us!"

Scanning our bookshelves to see if any other volumes would suddenly come to life and fling themselves to the ground, instead, to my horror, I watched the self-portrait of Van Gogh twist itself upon the wall as a boom of thunder crashed outside.

"Yes!" Holmes was in an ecstasy of joy. "You're doing splendidly, my dear! Now make your way towards Edison's machine. We kept it here for you! Try to pass between the box and the photoelectric cell so that you may speak to us!"

We all turned to stare at the red bulb atop Edison's Ghost Machine, a bulb that had never once lit up in all the time that it had been here…until now. To my utter astonishment, it began to glow. Slowly at first, a faint sliver of light threading its way up the bulb's filament, then beginning to glow more strongly as lightning cracked against the windowpanes. Miss Chartier's fingernails were digging into my flesh as Edison positively quivered in joy next to me.

"Yes! It works! I knew it!"

"Amazing!" marvelled Tesla. "Wonderful! It is beyond wonderful!"

"And now," continued Holmes, "we must solve your murder. Let me ask you some questions. One blink of the light means yes. Two means no. Do you understand?"

As the red bulb turned off and then back on, I felt my grip on reality and sanity beginning to unravel. Glancing at Miss Chartier, I could read the shock and disbelief in her eyes. Outside, the storm was shrieking as if the end of the world were upon us—thunder rolling and rain lashing against the window in sheets. Everything about this was wrong and unnatural, and I stood up from the table.

"Holmes!!! For God's sake, you must stop this! I don't know what you've done, what spirit or demon you have summoned from Hell, but it is not Irene Adler!"

As I pointed at Edison's Ghost Machine, the red bulb dimmed and went out.

"But it is! It must be!" said Edison. "She is communicating with us!"

Flinging my chair back, I hurried towards the lights and turned them on. "I'm putting an end to this!"

"You can't!" shouted Edison. "Let her speak!"

"This is science!" agreed Tesla. "We must continue!"

And then, above all of the cacophony came Miss Chartier's voice, clear and strong.

"Stop! All of you. Just stop."

By way of emphasis, she picked up the Mauser as a long, receding roll of thunder told us that the storm had passed over us. A steady patter of rain fell against the window as we all stared at Miss Chartier. Edison and Tesla were both flushed with excitement as Holmes sat motionless like the Sphinx, his expression and eyes completely inscrutable. Getting to her feet, Miss Chartier gazed around the room, from the books on the floor, to Van Gogh's self-portrait, to Edison's Ghost Machine. Hiking up her dress, she deposited the Mauser into a leg holster, and then looked at us with a wry smile.

"We are being played, gentlemen."

Edison was indignant. "What are you talking about? This is no game! My machine works! We all witnessed it!"

Miss Chartier picked up the Tesla coil, looked at it closely, and then handed it to Tesla, where it continued to hum and crackle in his hands.

"No. I have plotted my own share of little charades in my time, and I recognise one when I see it. Most beautifully planned and executed, I must say..."

"Miss Chartier," began Tesla, "I am afraid I do not understand what you are saying. I am a scientific man, yes, but I know that the miracles of the universe greatly exceed what we currently perceive and understand."

"I'm sure they do, but in my experience most miracles have a helping hand," returned Miss Chartier, before turning to me. "Dr. Watson, what has Mr. Holmes been up to these past two days?"

"The devil if I know!" I answered truthfully. "He's been up at all hours, running here and there to God knows where, doing God knows what, sending me on wild goose chases all over England..." I picked up one of the scientific journals. "...and I think he's read every word Tesla has ever written!"

Miss Chartier nodded. "As I suspected. For anything one man can discover, so too can another man. And there is our answer."

"What answer?" asked Tesla, and I must admit that I was as confused as he was. Normally, sitting in our rooms with Holmes, I am quite confident of my place and function in the grand scheme of things. But now, for whatever reason, Holmes had fallen silent, and it was Miss Chartier who was taking on the role of detective and endeavouring to deduce her way to a truth that was unclear to me.

"This is my third encounter with the formidable Mr. Holmes," continued Miss Chartier, "and I assure you that he is a most singular and exceptional man. But this...oh, what a masterpiece of cunning and deceit...orchestrated to perfection to achieve the desired effect. You would have made a superb criminal, Mr. Holmes."

At this, Holmes inclined his head in unspoken acknowledgement, and I had to admit that I had expressed much the same sentiment in the past. But was Miss Chartier implying that Holmes had committed some kind of crime?

"Miss Chartier," I began, "I demand to know precisely what it is that you are insinuating about Holmes."

"There is no need to demand. You say that Mr. Holmes immersed himself in the writings of Tesla, which means, of course, that he familiarised himself with Tesla's work in any number of fields. Radio, x-rays, but most especially, Tesla's work on remote control, or telautomatics as it is sometimes called; that is, the science of operating mechanisms at a distance."

"Why yes, I believe Holmes did mention that," I said.

"Wait..." At the mention of his own work, Tesla had become remarkably attentive. "What are you suggesting? That Mr. Holmes used remote control to activate Edison's Ghost Machine! No! That would be impossible! The remote control switches must be manually operated, and we were all holding hands at the table when Miss Adler showed herself!"

"And what about that painting moving," added Edison, "or those books falling off the shelves? Impossible!"

"No." Miss Chartier gave a small shake of her head. "Far from it. In fact, allow me to quote the great Mr. Holmes, 'When you have eliminated the impossible, whatever remains, however improbable, must be the truth.'"

Without another word, Miss Chartier whipped the tablecloth off the table and then in a single motion flipped the table over. Immediately, I could see that three small mechanisms had been secured on the underside of the table.

"Good God," I exclaimed. "What are those?"

"Why, they are remote control switches!" declared Tesla.

"Yes, that is exactly what they are," said Miss Chartier. "Switches powered by the wireless electricity provided by the Tesla coil, and the resourceful Mr. Holmes was able to operate them using only his feet, with none of us the wiser as we all held hands at the table. Consider that the darkened room covered his movements, and the sounds from Tesla's coil and the thunderstorm obscured any unusual noises. Observe..."

Miss Chartier proceeded to toggle one of the switches with her foot and the Van Gogh painting straightened itself on the wall. Reaching with the toe of her boot for another switch, the red light on Edison's box came back to life. She turned to Tesla.

"You may turn your coil off, Mr. Tesla."

As Tesla obediently shut down the Tesla coil, it ceased to hum and spark, and the red bulb atop Edison's Ghost Machine went dark.

"No…" Edison looked positively sick. "…so it was all just a trick…just a damned trick…"

I whirled on Holmes. "What's the meaning of this? To make fools of us? Is this your idea of sport? Why should you do such a thing?"

"Merely an experiment." Holmes made his way to the mantel and set a match to his cherry-wood pipe. "And yes, I will confess that I fully availed myself of Mr. Tesla's 1898 patent—Method and Apparatus for Controlling Mechanisms at a Distance. How much do I owe you for this little exhibition, Mr. Tesla? I have no wish to fall afoul of the U.S. Patent Office."

"Not a thing, Mr. Holmes," replied Tesla. "It was a most impressive demonstration."

"You're very kind. I do apologise for my little charade, as Miss Chartier put it, but I wished to see how everyone would react to Miss Adler's return from the grave. As it turned out, Mr. Edison and Mr. Tesla were swept away in raptures of delight at witnessing the valve between two worlds opening. On the other hand, Miss Chartier and Dr. Watson had quite a different reaction. Indeed, Dr. Watson feared that we were being visited by demons from beyond because he knew that I was not in contact with the deceased Irene Adler. How could he possibly know that with such perfect conviction? Curious, wouldn't you say? But he was sure of that for one very simple reason—Irene Adler is not dead."

The hush in the room was broken a moment later as our door swung open and there stood a dark figure covered head to foot in a black mackintosh still glistening from the rain. For one deranged moment I thought I was staring at the Grim Reaper, but then the figure took a step forward and the mackintosh fell away to reveal Miss Adler herself. This was no ghost or spirit, but the very real woman whose grave Sherlock Holmes had visited only yesterday. Silently, we all watched her as she approached Holmes and then stopped two feet short of him. For a long moment, they simply looked at one another. It was Holmes who spoke first.

"It's lovely to see you again, my dear."

"Likewise," answered Miss Adler.

"If I recall correctly, it was only a few short days ago that you expressed the wish to have your Sherlock back. Well, you've just seen my detective work in 'The Adventure of the Electrocuted Contralto.' Does it meet with your approval?"

By way of answer Miss Adler took Holmes in her arms and they embraced one another tightly for a good thirty seconds, until she pulled her head back to look at him.

"Are you angry with me?" she asked.

"Not at all. Everyone fakes their own death at some point."

As they smiled at one another, I felt obliged to render an objection. "I'm not sure that's entirely true."

Miss Adler disengaged herself from Holmes to regard him head to foot. "This is the man I fell in love with," she began. "Brilliant, inventive, and absolutely remorseless in his search for the truth."

"And this is the woman I fell in love with," returned Holmes. "Brilliant, inventive, and the genius behind this conspiracy."

Miss Adler turned to look at us. "Sherry, anyone?"

This suggestion was universally endorsed, and as she moved to the sideboard to get the sherry and glasses, she glanced at me. "And Dr. Watson, a fire would be lovely, don't you think?"

This was effectively a royal command, and as I speedily made my way to the fireplace, Miss Adler turned her attention back to Holmes. "I suspected it would come to this. I might even say that I hoped it would, which is why I wanted to be nearby while you conducted your séance. But now you must tell me, what gave it away?"

This was an invitation that Holmes could hardly decline, and as everyone took their seats to watch the performance, Miss Adler passed out glasses of sherry. Taking centre stage in the room, his hands clasped behind his back, Holmes indulged himself in a dramatic pause, revelling in the kind of moment that he hadn't experienced in some time.

"What gave it away, my dear? Trifles, of course. It began the morning when I prepared a lovely breakfast of coddled eggs and toast only to be told that I had become soft and complacent due to being in love with you. England and various clients needed Sherlock Holmes to be at the top of his game, so the current situation could not possibly be allowed to continue. Asking me to not love you was out of the question, so a different answer was required, and indeed, a different answer was found thanks to the invention of Nikola Tesla and the presence of Miss Chartier.

"I imagine it went something like this—after I had failed to make any headway with the devices of Mr. Tesla and Mr. Edison, you and Dr. Watson departed our rooms under the premise that I needed time alone to think. You then subsequently rendezvoused with my brother Mycroft to address what we shall call The Problem of Sherlock. What to do? And it was there within the hallowed halls of the Diogenes Club that the conspiracy was hatched, and it was decided that Irene Adler must die for the sake of the British Empire. Who would commit the murder? None other than the most dangerous criminal in Europe—Marie Chartier—who no doubt received assurances from Mycroft that her various crimes and indiscretions would be forgiven if she would play her part. Everyone was sworn to secrecy and fully on board with the plan."

Holmes paused to pick up Tesla's Death Ray. "And here, ready at hand, was the perfect weapon, which Mycroft no doubt deduced could be made functional whenever Mr. Tesla wished it to become functional. And it was in these very rooms, when he was threatening Mr. Edison with the device, that Tesla himself informed us it was capable of generating one hundred thousand volts of electricity. A lethal dose to be sure, but wait, here the first troublesome trifle raised its head. In the Chicago World's Fair demonstration witnessed by Miss Adler, as she told us, Tesla had two hundred thousand volts pass through his body, twice as many as produced by this weapon, and yet he was completely unharmed.

"How did he manage this? And it's here that our second trifle comes into play; specifically, the measurement of one inch. I will confess to being a little slow on this crucial point, but then, I had just witnessed the love of my life being murdered in cold blood, and my logical faculties were considerably disordered. But there was something off when Miss Adler returned after her long day out in London. I can't say that I registered it consciously, but it most definitely made an impact on my subconscious. True, she had purchased a most becoming new outfit, all the way from her hat down to her new boots, but it wasn't just that. What was different about her?

"And it was only by running events through my mind over and over that it finally came to me—somehow, she had grown one inch taller. Why? How? Well, let us consider Mr. Tesla's ability to withstand lethal doses of electricity. How did he accomplish this? A little research amongst various scientific journals revealed that high frequency alternating current of great voltages will flow largely on the outer surface of the skin without injury if one's shoes are sufficiently insulated to prevent grounding. What was your choice of insulating material, my dear? Cork or rubber?"

"One inch of black rubber," answered Miss Adler.

"Just so," continued Holmes. "With preparations complete, it was now time for a three-part drama to unfold. First upon the stage was Miss Chartier, a woman who has presented herself in many guises in furtherance of her various plots and schemes. This was a new role for her, that of murderess. Even considering her chequered past, it was a part that took nerves of steel, and she passed it with flying colours—taking hold of the Death Ray and firing it directly at Miss Adler as instructed.

"Now came the second part of the drama. Miss Adler collapsed dramatically to the floor, like the true veteran of many tragic operas that she is. Not over or underdone, her death was perfectly naturalistic and believable, and would no doubt have received the plaudits of the critics had it been performed onstage before a full house in the West End.

"And then it was time for the third act to bring the drama to a close. My good friend and colleague Dr. Watson now took his turn upon the boards like a true veteran of the stage. Kneeling next to the prostrate form of Miss Adler, he made a show of administering some kind of reviving tonic, which simply ran down Miss Adler's cheek and onto the floor. He then proceeded to take her wrist, feeling for a pulse, which was no doubt strong and rapid beneath his fingers. However, convincingly assembling his features into a mask of horror mingled with grief, he looked up at me and pronounced Miss Adler dead. Masterfully done, Watson. I must say, I was completely taken in."

"Thank you, Holmes," I murmured, feeling a sudden warmth in my cheeks.

"Ah, but that was a mistake," continued Holmes, "our third and final trifle, but one that I only realised from the manner in which Dr. Watson took my pulse as I lay on the divan. For a weak or undetectable pulse might indeed be the result of an illness or electric shock, so upon failing to find it in the wrist, any experienced doctor would then feel for a heartbeat in the carotid artery of the neck.

"This, my dear Watson, you failed to do, because once you felt the pulse in Irene's wrist, you knew she was not dead, and the curtain could be drawn on the entire sorry episode, with poor, grief-stricken Sherlock none the wiser. Irene Adler could now disappear into an unmarked grave, Sherlock Holmes would no longer be in love, and the British government and clients from around the globe would once again be able to rely on Sherlock Holmes to set the world right. End scene..."

Chapter Twelve
The More Things Change...

As he concluded his impressive deductive soliloquy, we all set down our sherry glasses to applaud, and Holmes acknowledged our ovation with a sweeping bow. When Miss Adler picked up her glass again, we all followed her lead.

"A toast to the great Sherlock Holmes. A man who has survived encounters not only with venomous snakes, violent criminals, and vicious hounds, but has now survived the most deadly threat he has ever encountered, the treacherous waters of romance, and the demonic possession of being in love."

We all drank to Holmes, and then Tesla took hold of his weapon.

"Well, allow me to say that I am greatly relieved that my Death Ray was not the cause of Miss Adler's demise. And I think, perhaps, it would be wise to discontinue any further research into a weapon such as this. In the wrong hands...it doesn't bear thinking about."

With that, Tesla removed the tungsten magnetron from the weapon and handed it to Holmes.

"Please accept this as a souvenir of the case. I will dispose of the rest of the device at my earliest convenience."

As Tesla packed his Death Ray back into its case, Edison picked up his Ghost Machine.

"And I'm sorry to say, the same goes for my device. Better to abandon it completely."

"But why?" I asked. "It might very well work. You can't let yourself be discouraged by Holmes' little trick."

Edison began putting his latest invention away.

"No. I am the inventor of the device and I was completely taken in by the séance. And do you know why? Because I wanted to be taken in…wanted to believe. True, there are many millions of dollars to be made preying on the hopes and fears of the gullible public, but that is a realm into which no reputable inventor ventures. I am not in the business of creating devices that rely on faith or delusion to make them work. A phonograph must play a song. A light must illuminate a room. This machine would be a goldmine for fakers and charlatans, and it would leave my reputation in tatters for all time. I can't risk it, and I won't. This is the last the world will see of Edison's Ghost Machine."

Just as Edison closed up his case with a solid click, Tesla did the same. They turned to one another, cases in hand, the two great rivals sizing each other up. And then I saw the hint of a smile cross Tesla's face.

"Buy you a drink, Tom?"

"Why not, Nikola? Why the hell not?"

"What new invention are you going to work on now?"

"Wouldn't you like to know?"

And if any of us were expecting long goodbyes or even the slightest acknowledgment from either Tesla or Edison, we were sorely disappointed. Once the topic of work had been raised, it was as if the rest of the world had disappeared, and so they made their way towards the door.

"You know," offered Tesla, "I have some thoughts regarding your Ghost Machine."

"Stop it."

"I will mull it over, and if I have a vision, I will let you know."

"I swear to God, Nikola, I'll build my own damned Death Ray..."

Immersed in their conversation, the last we heard of Edison and Tesla was them heading down the stairs and out into the night air of Baker Street.

Miss Adler finished her sherry and put down her glass.

"I'm leaving as well."

"Excellent!" enthused Holmes. "Where are we going?"

"You're not coming."

"What?" Holmes was genuinely shocked. "But Irene, you made your point! And quite brilliantly too, I might add. I have learned my lesson!"

Miss Adler merely shook her head, at which point Holmes redoubled his efforts.

"We'll take whatever cases you want! And I promise, no more gourmet breakfasts! It's cold porridge and weak tea every morning from now on!"

Again, Miss Adler shook her head, and an expression of despair spread across Holmes' features. "Irene...I can't lose you again."

"And you never will," answered Miss Adler as she picked up her book and opened it to the first page. "But I'm taking the advice of the opening lines of 'The Awakening.' *'Allez-vous-en! Allez-vous en! Sapristi!'* Go away. Go away, for God's sake."

"Go away where?" asked Holmes.

"I'm taking the train to Southampton and the next ocean liner to the United States. It will be nice to see New York again...and there are some upcoming roles at the Metropolitan Opera that I wouldn't mind auditioning for. As Miss Chartier said, 'A little resurrection never killed anyone.'"

During this entire exchange, Miss Chartier had simply stood there, silent and watchful. But at Miss Adler's mention of an ocean voyage, her interest was immediately piqued. "You are going to New York? Without Mr. Holmes?"

"Without Mr. Holmes," answered Miss Adler.

"Would you like some company?"

"Seriously?"

"I am not interested in being watched by Mycroft Holmes for the rest of my life. And this American banker, this J. P. Morgan, he fascinates me. Cruel, grasping, willing to destroy anyone in his path...he reminds me of my father, and I should very much like to meet him."

"Then pack your bags, Miss Chartier."

"*Bien!*" Miss Chartier turned with a smile. "Mr. Holmes. Dr. Watson. I am off to explore new fields of opportunity in America, and I very much look forward to not having my future plans foiled by you. And yet, I must admit..."

She trailed off, and Holmes nodded in understanding.

"I quite agree, Miss Chartier. I shall miss our little encounters as well."

"Well, maybe I'll just pop by New York someday," I offered. "Say hello...have a hot dog...some chewing gum...or whatever Americans eat..."

"I would enjoy that," answered Miss Chartier. "I would enjoy that very much indeed. But at least for the moment, *au revoir mes amis.*"

As Miss Chartier moved for the door and exited, Holmes turned to Miss Adler.

"Irene...I don't understand why you're doing this."

"Because I love you enough to let you be who you really are. Enough to leave you." Miss Adler gestured towards all the scientific books and journals scattered about the room. "Tell me the truth. These last few days, your investigation into my death...how did it make you feel?"

"It was exhilarating," answered Holmes. "Just like I remembered...like the old days...walking into the fog of uncertainty and making it clear through the gathering of data and then the pure application of implacable logic until the cold, hard light of the truth was revealed."

"Precisely. And that is who you are, my beautiful, beautiful detective." Miss Adler took Holmes into her arms and kissed him, then pulled away. "Time will pass. It will pass more quickly than you can imagine. Soon enough, you will retire to Sussex Downs to raise your beloved bees. And when you do, I will be there to raise them with you...and we will grow old together."

"Yes, my love," Holmes regarded her with his eyes shining, no longer arguing or disputing what she was doing, but simply accepting that this is what she wanted and the way it had to be.

When Miss Adler then turned to me, my mind went blank. She had been with us for so long, and had shared so many bizarre characters and adventures, that the prospect of her leaving seemed unthinkable. Would we have been able to help Vincent Van Gogh without her assistance, and uncovered Marie Chartier's diabolical plan to exploit the tortured lives of the Post-Impressionist painters? And what of the case involving Auguste Escoffier and Bertie, the Prince of Wales?

When they came to us in desperate circumstances, Escoffier was a talented chef, but also a common thief, stealing without any hint of remorse from his employers at The Savoy Hotel. Now he was the head chef at the Ritz Hotel in Paris and acclaimed as the greatest culinary genius of his age. As for

Bertie, he had arrived at 221B as the gambling and womanising Prince of Wales, the notorious Playboy Prince as he was known, but his experiences in our rooms had left him a changed man, so that from the moment he ascended the throne as Edward VII in 1901, he proved to be both a wise and beloved King. Would all of that have transpired without the presence and influence of Miss Adler? I seriously doubt it. In short, European history as we know it owed her a considerable debt, even if she had operated largely behind the scenes. Looking at one another now, we were both lost for words.

"For God's sake, John..." she finally said in a voice choked with emotion. "Say something..."

Dubious of my ability to say anything remotely articulate given the size of the lump in my throat, all I could manage was a weak wave of my hand and a snatch of song.

"Give my regards to Broadway..."

Simultaneously, two tears burst from her eyes and trickled down both cheeks, and then, one kiss on my cheek later, she was gone. Holmes and I stood in shock at everything that had just transpired, our very lives flung about like ragdolls from one moment to the next. But then, that is the nature of existence should you have both the fortune and misfortune of living long enough. You assume that your life is one thing, until the moment that it isn't.

"I'm sorry, Holmes. I'm so sorry."

"Don't be. She's right, of course. As always. But perhaps I will just move my retirement plans up a few months..."

Knowing there would never be a better time to broach the subject, I took a deep breath and plunged in. "Are you angry with me?"

"Angry?" Holmes was refilling his pipe. "Oh, you mean for being my closest friend in the world and conspiring against me? For engaging in an elaborate hoax designed to convince me that the woman I love was dead?"

"Yes," I answered. "If you would prefer that I move out and cease all association with you, I quite understand."

"Don't be ridiculous." Holmes lit his pipe. "You know very well that I would be lost without you. You were doing your duty, and doing it to the best of your ability. Your actions were, in fact, heroic. Not thinking of yourself, but thinking of the greater good. And I must say you carried it off wonderfully."

That was all I needed to hear, and the subject was never raised again. And here, I might pause a moment for a brief apology to the reader who has followed this tale. I might very well be accused of "not playing fair" in terms of telling this story, but I would beg to point out that not once did I utter a lie or untruth insofar as the reader was concerned. The most I can be accused of is being in possession of certain facts and not being inclined to share them because of the deleterious effect it would have had on the narrative. And if all that is not enough, well, all I can say is *mea culpa*!

"And now it is my turn to ask the same question," said Holmes. "Are you angry with me?"

"For?"

"Borrowing an idea from 'Hamlet' and feigning a little bit of madness to help explain the rather ridiculous yet necessary devices I employed to get you out of our rooms for extended periods of time."

"Oh, you mean my lonely dinner at Simpson's and my pointless journey to Liverpool."

"As well as your expedition to get me a new magnifying lens and my insistence that you walk everywhere so it would take you as long as possible. My preparations for a séance enlivened by remote control devices required your extended absence, I'm afraid."

"I can imagine," I concurred. "And quite a compelling exhibition, I might add."

"You're very kind to say so, but I was simply applying the information that I found in Tesla's patents and journal articles."

As this was clearly the time to ask and answer whatever questions might be on our minds, I had one final concern.

"Tell me honestly, Holmes. Are you going to be all right?"

"Well, I have to be, don't I? I am Sherlock Holmes, after all. And Sherlock Holmes needs a brandy."

"Excellent idea!" I agreed, heading to the sideboard. "I'll join you."

As I poured two snifters, Holmes moved to the window and looked out into the night.

"What do you think the future holds, Holmes?" I asked. "Tesla may have been dissuaded from fully developing his Death Ray, but surely there are other inventors out there right now, doing their best to build some new device to massacre other human beings with even greater efficiency. Every day, it seems as if the world becomes a darker and darker place...people tearing at one another's throats for no good reason...or simply because they're told to."

"Sadly true," answered Holmes. "Do you know that the Germans have a word for anyone who isn't German? *Auslander*. And the Japanese have a word for anyone who isn't Japanese. *Gaijin*. The Armenians have a word for anyone who isn't Armenian. *Odar*. We're a tribal species, Watson. And no doubt if you asked your new friend Mr. Darwin, he would tell you that our tribalism was a trait that was naturally selected for back in the Stone Age. We survived because of it. But that was back when our weapons were sticks and stones. Now, with weapons like those of Mr. Tesla we have become little more than great apes with Death Rays, and I fear that very same tribalism will be the end of us. Unless the day comes soon when we can look across a room, a continent, or an ocean, and simply see other human beings not all that different from ourselves, we won't be long for this world."

As I handed Holmes his brandy, he took a thoughtful sip and then continued.

"In short, we're a barely sentient group of apes who wandered off the savanna, on a little ball of rock and water, on the edge of a medium-sized galaxy. All we have is ourselves... and too many of our fellow humans, in their fear and ignorance, are ready to eradicate one another for almost any reason at all. That is what we must stand against. The chaos of the human condition and the inhumanity of man against man. And so we shall continue in our noble efforts, my friend, not minding the bad and foolish world."

"Well, that can only mean thing..." Moving to the mantel, I pulled the jackknife from the pile of letters from prospective clients and waved them in the air. "We need a case!"

"Indeed we do," agreed Holmes. "Now, I think we can cross off the Foreign Office's fears regarding Germany acquiring Tesla's Death Ray, so let's stop by Scotland Yard tomorrow to see how Lestrade's getting on with the Abernathy poisoning case...after our trip to Hampstead."

"Hampstead? Why are we going to Hampstead?"

"To find Lady Bracknell's lost puppy, of course."

As Holmes took his seat in the armchair and sipped his brandy, I sat near him on the divan and tried to compose my thoughts as best I could.

"Holmes, there's something I want to tell you. We've been through any number of cases together, and encountered the most bizarre mysteries and astonishing characters and creatures over the years, whether it was 'The Adventure of the Musgrave Ritual,' 'Black Peter,' or the Sholto twins in 'The Sign of the Four.' We've shared a number of triumphs, and yes, we both know that there have been some darker moments as well. But there is nothing that I treasure, nothing that I value more, than simply having the honour of being your friend. Steel true, blade straight, you are the best and wisest man I have ever known."

Holmes leaned back in his chair, raised his eyes to the ceiling, and after a good thirty seconds said something I know he would have never said had it not been for the salutary influence of Irene Adler. "I love you too, Watson."

Holmes proceeded to raise his glass, and I did likewise.

"I'm going to say it," I said.

"Of course you are."

"The game is afoot!"

We clinked our glasses together.

"Elementary, my dear Watson. Elementary."

And as we sipped our brandies and stretched our feet out towards the fire, I knew with absolute certainty that there was nothing more that I desired in this world than to venture out to Hampstead in the morning in search of a lost puppy...with my good friend Sherlock Holmes by my side.

The End.